I0824169

MY
Wonderful
DISGRACE

**To anyone who's ever had a bad night.**
**AR**

**To the graduating class of Richmond River High School, 1986. And to EJ K-B, who deserved better.**
**KR**



First US edition 2026
First published by Walker Books Australia 2026

Library of Congress Control Number: pending
ISBN 978-1-5362-4743-5

26 27 28 29 30 31 SHD 10 9 8 7 6 5 4 3 2 1

Printed in Chelsea, MI, USA

This book was typeset in Adobe Garamond.

Candlewick Press
99 Dover Street
Somerville, Massachusetts 02144

www.candlewick.com

EU Authorized Representative: HackettFlynn Ltd,
36 Cloch Choirneal, Balrothery, Co. Dublin, K32 C942, Ireland.
EU@walkerpublishinggroup.com

# My Wonderful Disgrace

ANGOURIE RICE
AND KATE RICE

CANDLEWICK PRESS

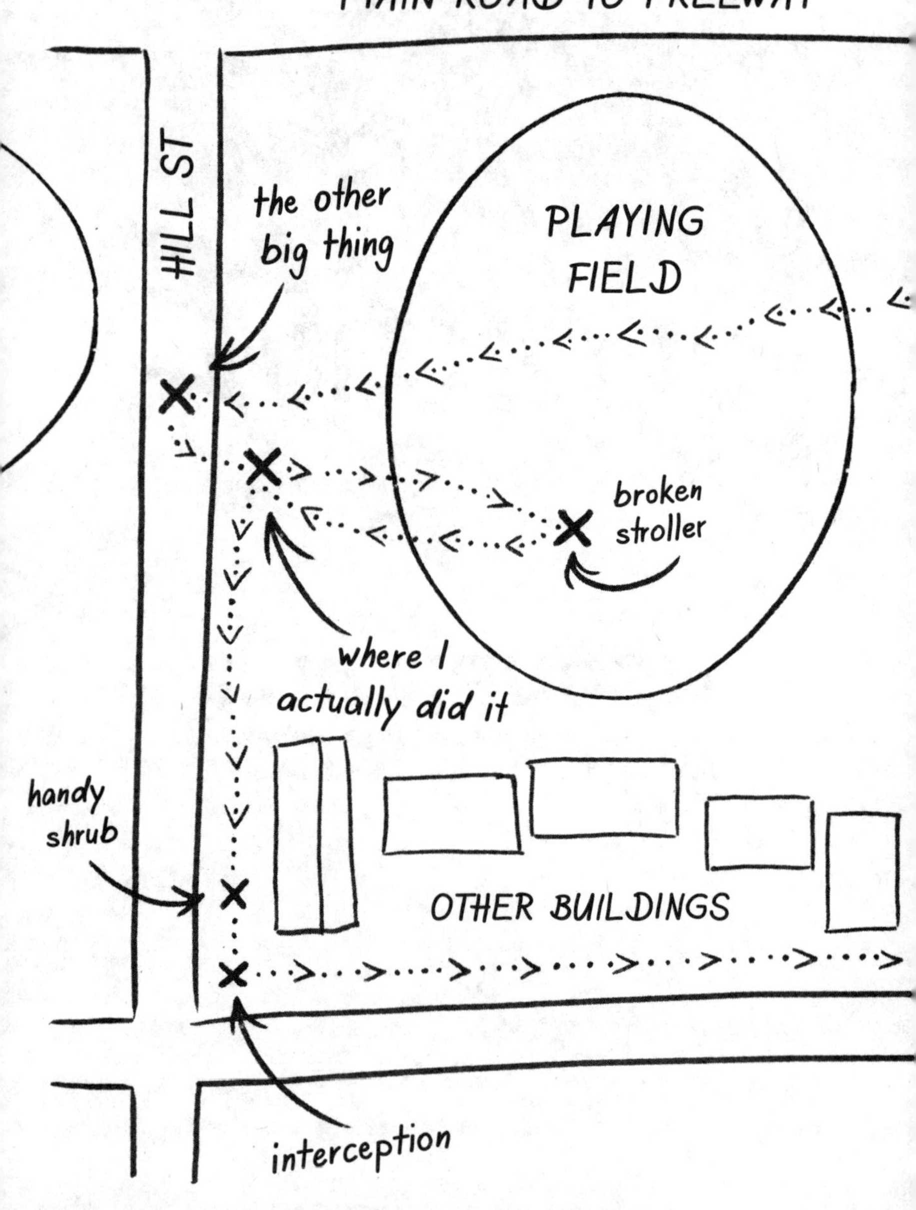
MAIN ROAD TO FREEWAY
HILL ST
the other big thing
PLAYING FIELD
broken stroller
where I actually did it
handy shrub
OTHER BUILDINGS
interception

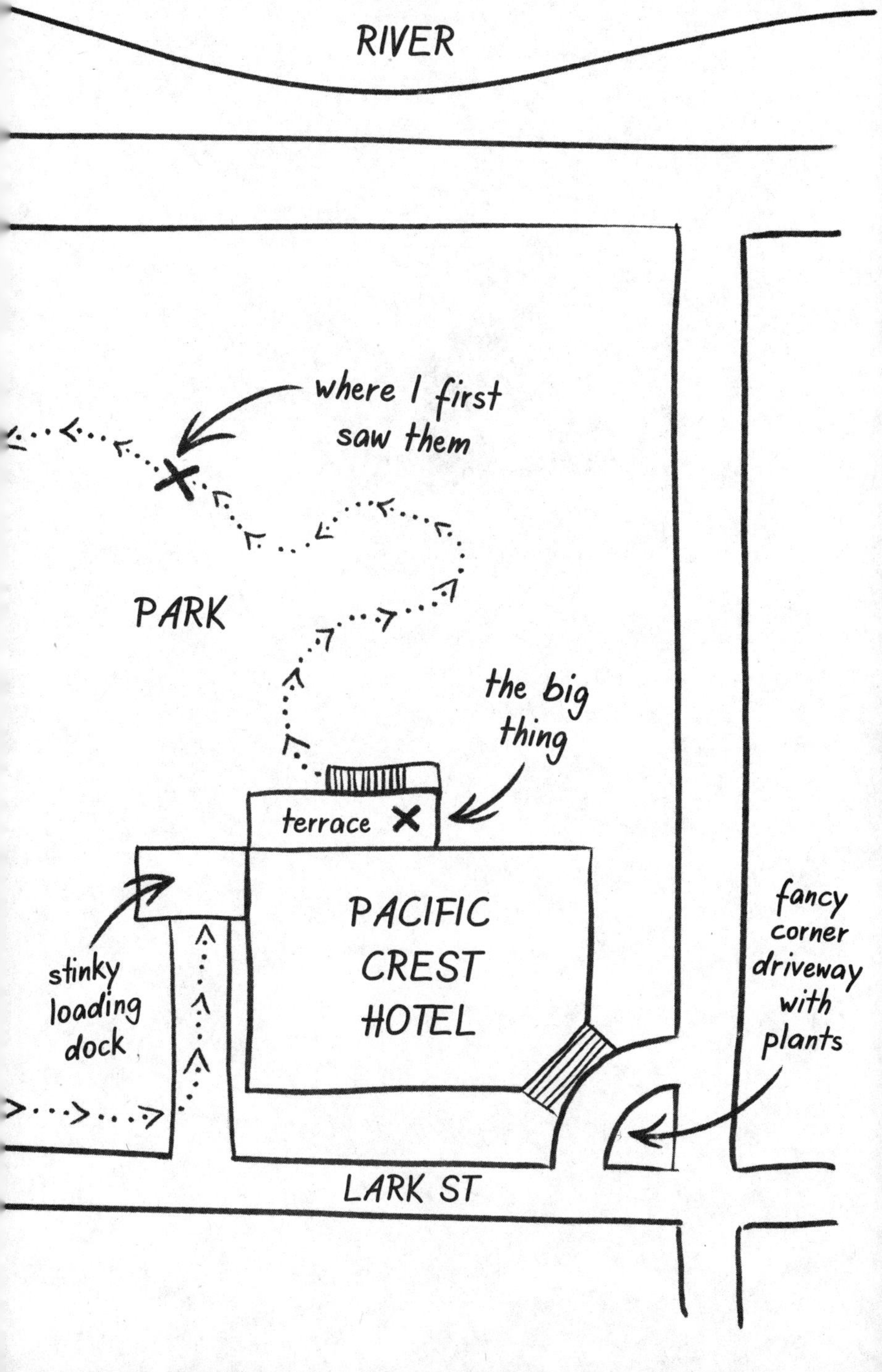

RIVER

where I first saw them

PARK

the big thing

terrace

PACIFIC CREST HOTEL

stinky loading dock

fancy corner driveway with plants

LARK ST

1

## AMY'S JOURNAL—SUNDAY

So. The ball is five days away, which is either a long time or no time at all, depending on how ready you are. And you know me. I prepare. Spent most of today workshopping hair; have chosen a half-up-half-down with a bit of braiding and *sooo* many hairpins but it totally works and honestly, six hours later it's still holding up. Dress is in the closet and every so often I open the door and just touch it because PRETTY. I also practiced shoe-wearing today, identified where they bite so I know where to stick the gel Band-Aids (basically everywhere). Went to the mall, purchased gel Band-Aids. Also purchased a new highlighter sparkle stick just like Bianca's, even though she said I could borrow it and I can't really afford one. (This is not summer camp. Germs.) Appetizers are sorted, limo is booked, presentation speech is ready to go. So truly, Everything Is Awesome.

Except.

I have no date. Which is totally not awesome and is completely and categorically effed up. Nobody asked me. No one. Not even Bevan! Yes I've ignored/rejected him for six years, but we're still friends, and it would have been so adorably sweet for him to ask me to the ball. Lucky he didn't, to be honest; in my current state I may have actually said yes. Because you don't dream about your school ball for your entire life and then turn up without a date. School ball is fantasy fulfillment. It's about the dress, it's about the hair, it's about crossing that threshold into adult life, your first ride in a limo, and, of course, THE BOY. And I say that as an empowered feminist. I am strong, I am powerful, and I want to go to the ball with a boy I like. In that way. He's tall, he's fun, we get each other, we have the best time ever, and sometime during this amazing evening he totally realizes he's in love with me and he's ALWAYS been in love with me. We kiss in a cloud of twinkles and bursting love hearts and this is the beginning of the best love story ever.

Can you guess? Of course you can.

I would write his name down but I'm too scared because he hasn't asked me, he's never going to ask me, I'm going to be a loser girl supporting other people having a terrible time with their dates. And I don't know what to do about it.

Pray for me.

**Group Chat: Amy, Gabby, Kate, Bianca, Veronika**
**Sunday, April 9**

**Gabby:** R u guys doing nails?

**Kate:** Yes. And wax

**Gabby:** Where?

**Kate:** At the mall

**Gabby:** No like where on ur body

**Kate:** Everywhere

**Amy:** Remember we're doing this because we want to, not for any man

**Bianca:** Do you think Fred will like my hair best up or down?

**Chat: LochNess, Devinitely**
**Sunday, April 9**

**LochNess:** So?

**Devinitely:** Working on it

**LochNess:** Work harder

**Devinitely:** I am!

**LochNess:** Harder than that. Like how hard I'm nagging. That hard.

**Devinitely:** That's pretty hard

**LochNess:** I commit

## AMY'S JOURNAL—MONDAY

Okay. Bianca and Kate and Gabby sat me down at recess today and gave me a right good old talking-to. Here is what we all established together:

1. We don't need boys to have a good time. We are not like Crystal and her gang. We are invincible, incredible, amazing women with amazing lives and our happiness does not depend on attention from anyone of the male persuasion. F that S.

2. If we do happen to want a boy just as an accessory—as a kind of perfect handbag to the outfit that is already perfect—then we are permitted to go and find one ourselves. We do not need to sit back and wait to be offered what we want. We go out and take what we want because we deserve it and we can.

3. If you're friends with someone, and they happen to identify as male, and you are mature and they are mature, then asking them out for a special occasion should totally not be a big deal and will in no way threaten your friendship or the possibility that maybe one day there might conceivably be something more than friendship on the horizon, if we're lucky, not that I'm even thinking about that because goodness I don't have time for a boyfriend right now anyway.

4. Boys are not very good at thinking ahead or deeply about anything. It is quite possible that a particular boy who actually wants to go to the ball with a particular girl might not have applied the right amount of brain power to such a thing yet, even though it's only four sleeps away and it's kind of slipped his mind that he still has to ask her.

5. I'm going to ask him tomorrow.

(6. Yes I'm quietly terrified, no girl should ever have to go through this so close to the ball, but feminism.)

(7. Also, I am categorically, genuinely, absolutely, most definitely not *in love* with Leo Prince. However, I do really really really like him. And now that I've written his name in my journal, I am the absolute definition of ridiculous. I'm going to smarten myself up and read some Virginia Woolf before bed.)

**Anonymous Love Letter Posted in Year 12 Group Chat**
**Monday, April 10**

To: Amy
From: Your school ball date?

Giving up is not something I do.
A place in my heart will always be reserved for you.
Believe me.
Because someday I'll have the courage to tell you that I love you.

Yours truly,
—Secret Admirer

P.S. I hope you can figure out who I am but if not that's ok I'll be waiting ☺

## AMY'S JOURNAL—TUESDAY

Omigodomigodomigodomigod. So. Here's what went down.

I followed him out of Math and down the hallway. So romantic—dodging loud stinky Year 8s and backpacks.

"So do you have a date for the ball?" (I knew he didn't.)

"Not really—thought I'd just go with Macca."

"I'm having a pre-ball cocktail party at my place if you'd like to come? Fred will be there." (Bianca's boyfriend. I may not have mentioned him before. He's a bit of a dick but they've been together since Year 9 and she really likes him so he can't be all bad.)

He asked, "You really want Macca at your place?" Macca is a party animal and a vomiter.

"Oh, maybe not Macca. It'll just be a few of us . . . Bianca and Kate and—"

"But I'm going in Macca's limo."

"You could come in ours. With me."

"Yeah—I guess I could—but I've already chipped in," he said. I had just ripped my heart out and presented it to him, still pumping and dripping, and he was worried about whether he'd get his fifty bucks back. Seriously?

"Anyway, think about it. I don't have a date yet, so . . ." Drift off, cheeks pink, look awkward. My god. And he was looking straight at me, sadly NOT in the way that would suggest he was falling hopelessly in love. More in the way that suggested he was still thinking about the fifty bucks. No matter, the answer is deep in my eyes, Leo, keep gazing. Is my mascara holding up? Are you suddenly realizing how bewitchingly pretty I am? Or am I the only person falling deeper in love right now because you're just looking so . . . tousled. Dammit, why are you so attractive???

*DING*—his phone went off, the spell was broken, and he was gone. Catch you later, yeah whatever. You really have to squeeze life in between those dings.

By the time I got back to the girls, I was almost in tears.

I collapsed into Gabby and Bianca and Kate's collective arms and sympathy and babbled. Finally they got out of me what actually happened, and they thought I didn't actually ask—I hinted heavily, which I maintain is pretty much the same thing, but Bianca, who obviously has the most experience with such things, says it's not. For all their mysterious confidence, it's true—guys can be pretty thick. I was totally convinced I had just put myself right out there and he had turned me down, but the girls thought he probably didn't even get what I was saying. He probably thought it was just a casual conversation about casual things. I would have to be more clear. If I were clear, they said, of course the answer would be yes. Because they are my friends.

"You could get any guy you wanted," Bianca said.

"Then why don't I HAVE one?" I lamented.

"Because guys are stupid," declared Kate.

"What about the anonymous love letter poem?" said Gabby. "Your mystery admirer? I mean, if it's not Leo . . ."

"It's Bevan," chorused absolutely everyone. We hadn't even discussed it. No need.

"And I'm not going with him," I added.

"Then go with me," said Gabby. Which was sweet of her. "Like as your date." She is so nice to me but seriously she is going to have to work on being a bit less of a doormat. I mean, that's kind of what I love about her and I try not to take advantage—we have been BFFs for absolutely ever—but I don't want a sympathy date OR to confuse the public about my sexual identity. I'm Amy Middleton, I specialize in straight, and I definitely don't want to scare Leo off at this point.

And then it happened.

*Ding.*

**HEY WHY DON'T WE GO TO THE BALL TOGETHER—BE FUN.**

From Leo! Yes it was! No lie, this is exactly what he said. What it lacked in romance it made up for in directness. No equivocation, no beating around the bush, no need to breathlessly decipher what he meant (which we often have to do with Fred's texts. Sorry Bianca). I hinted, he accepted, we are ON.

"Typical!" said Kate.

"Guys always do that," said Bianca. "I told you you could have anyone you wanted."

Just like that—from the depths of despair to the dizzying heights of ecstasy all in the space of one short text message. Everything is falling into place. Finally.

SCHOOL COMMUNITY NEWSLETTER

## FROM THE PRINCIPAL'S DESK

On behalf of the entire staff and student body of our school, I would like to wish the Year Twelves all the best for the upcoming school ball. It is a significant milestone in your school life, and indeed in your journey to adulthood, and one that will be fondly remembered in years to come.

I would like to remind all students, parents, and guardians that the school ball is scheduled early in the academic year in order to allow students to enjoy themselves without inordinate impact on their studies. That said, even though it is only April, your schoolwork should always take precedence. The school ball is a privilege and an extracurricular activity, NOT a right nor an excuse to neglect your academic, athletic, and family obligations.

In addition, and I'm sorry this has to be said, but it is not necessary or desirable to spend vast amounts of money on designer fashion, grooming paraphernalia, or transportation. This is not an exercise in showing off, and I hope that we as a school community have fostered an inclusive attitude that values character above appearance. It is perfectly acceptable to arrive at the ball in the family car, and nice, affordable, appropriate clothing items are readily available at places like a discount department store.

I would also like to remind all concerned that this is a celebration outside of school hours, and while every effort will be made by the school to ensure the event runs smoothly, those who choose to participate do so at their own risk.

The schedule for the evening is as follows:

• 6:00 p.m. Arrival at the Pacific Crest Hotel on Lark Street, downtown. Early arrivals are not encouraged. Those wishing to drop off may do so, but please be aware there is a strict policy of *two minutes only* in the driveway. In the past we have had difficulty with parents leaving their cars to take photos. You must remain with your vehicle at all times and move on in a timely manner to avoid congestion. May I suggest a comprehensive photo session prior to your arrival.

• 6:10 p.m.–6:40 p.m. Drinks and appetizers served in the upper foyer area. Please make your way to the upper foyer on arrival. There are other hotel guests using the lower foyer so please be mindful that this is *not* an appropriate area to congregate. The upper foyer will have a pop-up portrait studio by Too Cool For School Photography. Portraits may be purchased online following the event.

• 6:40 p.m. The buffet will open in the upper foyer area, and you may commence dinner. Please line up to be served and carry your plate (carefully!) back to your table inside the adjacent ballroom. There is a seating plan. A lot of effort has gone into its arrangement and this has been available on the Intranet for two weeks now, so please *do not swap* seats unless you have a prior agreement to do so. I also suggest you identify your seat *before* you get your food as the ballroom is large with well over twenty tables; you don't want to be wandering around with a full plate.

• 8:00 p.m. Presentation by Class President Amy Middleton. There will be a speech and slideshow presentation celebrating your years together as a school community, and in the past this has always been a highlight of the evening.

• 8:15 p.m. Dancing begins and dessert buffet opens.

• 10:00 p.m. End of night. Please ensure you are collected on time or that you have made other appropriate arrangements. The cleaning staff require access at 10:15 p.m. sharp, and the venue must be fully vacated by that time. Be aware that due to safety concerns, we do not encourage the use of rideshare or similar services, but if they are used, please use caution and sensible judgment and if possible travel in pairs.

On a personal note, I would like to thank Amy Middleton and the School Ball Committee for their tireless efforts in preparing for this special event. I look forward to it myself each year and take great personal pride in seeing the majority of our students, many of whom I have known since Year Seven, conducting themselves at such a prestigious event as the delightful and mature young adults they have become.

## AMY'S JOURNAL—WEDNESDAY

Got a wax and a mani-pedi after school. Cost a hundred bucks. Beauty is expensive. Had to study until late so super tired. Stupid ball. They should put it on during the holidays when we've actually got time to do it properly.

Leo smiled at me in Math today.

Okay I am so embarrassed I even wrote that.

**Group Chat: Crystal, Tallulah, Jasi, Sumaya**
**Wednesday, April 12**

**Crystal:** Truly baffled Leo asked that wet sock to be his ball date

**Jasi:** I know! He hasn't dated anyone since year 10!

**Sumaya:** Going to a ball with someone doesn't mean you're dating

**Crystal:** Ha. Try telling Amy that.

## AMY'S JOURNAL—THURSDAY

Spent the whole afternoon/evening studying *The Great Gatsby* with a facial mask on. Can you believe they scheduled a test tomorrow so we have to show up to school? So frickin' rude. I tell you, if I ever grow up to be a teacher, which I obviously won't, I will never ever do anything like that. Of course it's an astounding novel and really clever and everything, but seriously, all we want to do is enjoy our party and they're ruining it by making us sit in a classroom and write an essay on a novel that's ALL ABOUT PARTYING. Not to mention unrequited love. It's just cruel. By the time we get home from school tomorrow, we'll only have two hours before appetizers. That is not enough time for amateurs to complete professional-looking hair and makeup. We will have to make do.

Meanwhile, ever since actually writing a certain person's name in here, and mentioning a certain person to my friends, I have become nothing short of obsessed. It's gross. And yet inevitable. The floodgates have opened and I can finally admit it: Leo's been my guy since forever. Seriously. Even through the whole disaster that was Year 9, and the additional blip that was Oliver Ransmann, Leo was always the one I liked. (Okay, just flipped back to the Oliver incident, and I know I sound like I'm wildly in love, but I was young then, okay? I've since grown up quite a bit and clearly become an entirely different person.) Leo's got charm, he's funny, he's cool, he's got that tousle of curls, skin like silk, eyes like a glass of clear water on a sunny terrace in the south of bloody France. And through no fault of my own, I have turned from a sensible person with a sincere yet charmingly theoretical interest in him to a full-on smitten kitten with a mighty crush. Just in the space of a couple of days. Am I going crazy? Or is this what a formal event does to a girl? Buy the dress and the ridiculousness will follow?

And yet, it's not ridiculous. It's actually supremely perfect. After however many years slogging it out at school in the most unromantic buildings, the ugliest uniforms, the most embarrassing situations, the hours of boredom, the countless episodes of everyday horror, we are finally getting our chance not as students or daughters or sons or athletes or violinists or whatever else everybody sees us as or wants us to be—we are now going to be real people. This is our moment to shine in the spotlight. In my case, quite literally. I'm doing the presentation speech to acknowledge achievements, welcome everyone to this new final phase of our schooling, thank the teachers and the school, blah-di-blah. It's actually really lovely and I've worked really hard on it with Principal Kruger. She wants me to make the school look like every parent's dream of academic achievement, artistic brilliance, and social harmony. My plan is to move every single person in the room to tears. I promise you there won't be a dry eye in the ballroom when I get to the bit about our shared past and our independent future. For better or worse, things will never be the same again. You only get one final year of school, and only one school ball.

And when I finish my speech, and I'm just standing in the spotlight in my Victor-Drummoyne-rose-quartz-mermaid-skirt-illusion-bodice-with-beaded-lace and the dance music starts, it will be Leo who leads me onto the dance floor and into the next stage of our lives. As adults. Together. I hope.

**Chat: LochNess, Devinitely**
**Thursday, April 13**

**LochNess:** So?

**Devinitely:** I've got something

**LochNess:** FINALLY

**Devinitely:** A friend of a friend came through

**LochNess:** Great

**Devinitely:** Don't you want to know how I did it?

**LochNess:** I don't care as long as you've got it

**Devinitely:** Fine. A magician never reveals his secrets anyway

**LochNess:** You're not the magician. You're the apprentice

**Devinitely:** Like Mickey in Fantasia

**LochNess:** Literally what are u on

**Devinitely:** Never mind

**Group Chat: Amy, Gabby, Kate, Bianca, Veronika**
**Friday, April 14, 11:30 p.m.**

**Gabby:** Amy r u ok?

**Kate:** If there's anything we can do, just let us know

**Bianca:** Yeah, we're totally here for u. Anything u need <3

## AMY'S JOURNAL—SATURDAY

FUCK FUCK FUCK FUCK **FUCK**.

MY LIFE IS FUCKED.

FUCK IT.

2

SCHOOL COMMUNITY NEWSLETTER

## FROM THE PRINCIPAL'S DESK

As many of you are aware, there was an unfortunate series of incidents at the school ball on Friday night that may have caused some distress. The events have alerted myself and the school to certain situations and there is currently an investigation underway. I ask at this time that you please refrain from speculation and innuendo as this is counterproductive to the morale of the school and highly inappropriate. Be assured that all matters raised are being dealt with by the appropriate authorities in a timely manner, and I will endeavor to keep the school community informed as required, bearing in mind our ongoing duty of care and respect for the privacy of the individuals involved in these matters. In the meantime:

- If you have any information you believe to be relevant to the investigation, please contact the school immediately and we will direct you to the appropriate officers.

• If your child requires counseling, please refer them to our Student Welfare Officer, Regina Armbruster, who can be contacted 9:00 a.m.–1:00 p.m. on Tuesdays and Thursdays in her office, and 3:00 p.m.–5:00 p.m. on Friday afternoons at her home via telephone or the Internet.

• We encourage all staff, students, and parents to review the following guidelines and resources that are available at all times through the school website. These are and have always been the school's official position on these matters.

—Bullying policy

—Behavior policy

—Dress code

• I have always prided myself on my approachability and accessibility as principal. I have an open-door policy and am happy to address any concerns you may still have in person as my availability allows. Please contact Administrative Support Officer Kimmbalee Ritchie to arrange a meeting.

## AMY'S JOURNAL—SUNDAY

Okay.

If I don't write this down now, I will block it from my memory and nobody will ever know the truth of the complete clusterfuck that was the best school ball ever. And as tempting as that is, I have too much respect for history, human relationships, and my own life to allow my experience of this episode to be erased. I've already experienced the worst. I've cried buckets of tears. Literally. No, not literally, but pretty much literally, to the point where I don't give a shit about the real meaning of the word "literally." Reliving it all here can't possibly be any more painful.

Probably the most painful bit is rereading what I wrote before. BB. Before Ball. It's like I can see some other Amy who looks a bit like me but is actually completely different, naive and sad, because she actually believes that the ball will live up to her unrealistic expectations. Or even just be normal. That person who was so excited and gushing . . . It's like someone pointing out that a ruffled blouse you like actually looks like a vagina. Once you see it, you can't unsee it. And when I look back at myself, all I see is vagina. I see one great big vagina, with a whole bunch of other vaginas, taking over the bathroom to do hair and makeup at three in the afternoon on a day that's too warm, in a room that's too small for three curling irons. I see way too much effort put into smoothing and highlighting and plucking and powdering. I see discussions about dresses and color matching and heels and tape, which seemed so important at the time, as just a little bit pointless and sad. I see all four of us giggling with champagne flutes: Gabby, with the face of an innocent angel, a halo of dark curls, in a '70s emerald-green halter-neck maxi; Bianca in a ruby-red strapless column; Kate in a black sweetheart-neckline ball gown with sparkles and cobalt-blue pumps. And me, in my Victor-fucking-Drummoyne-rose-fucking-quartz-mermaid-fucking-skirt-illusion-fucking-bodice-with-beaded-fucking-lace. (Sorry about the swearing.) Heavy but looks light as a feather, silver stilettos, silver clutch, half-up-half-down hair with braiding, and the feeling that absolutely nothing could ever go wrong ever again. And if it did, that it didn't matter. Because when Leo strolled out to join us on our back deck in a black suit that fit him like a glove and a boutonniere that matched the shade of my dress and the delicate bloom of love in my heart, my Life Was Perfect.

We should have ended the night then.

SCHOOL COMMUNITY NEWSLETTER

## FROM THE PRINCIPAL'S DESK

I am disappointed to report that there have been ongoing rumors and speculation about the incidents of the school ball. This has become apparent to me through countless meetings with staff, parents, and students over recent days, in which I have endeavored to be as transparent as possible, but I must insist that the school community respects the process and the privacy of those directly involved. I assure you that the school has at all times acted with the utmost integrity, and I can set the record straight here with regard to several matters that have been the subject of unfortunate conjecture, in order to clear up any misunderstandings. Please read the following very carefully before you call to arrange a meeting with me, as my time is limited and I'm getting very tired of repeating myself.

Administrative communication between the school and the hotel has at all times been professional and cordial. Administrative Support Officer Kimmbalee Ritchie has been dismayed and also rather hurt by suggestions she may have either by design or neglect had any responsibility for what happened. In fact, she went above and beyond in her communication with Events staff at the hotel, who I believe may have had internal communication problems of their own, but that's not for me to conjecture. I have personally sighted all copies of emails, etc., sent to the hotel and I can assure you that we had preapproval for an audiovisual presentation of the highest quality. Administrative Support Officer Kimmbalee is also swamped and she shouldn't have to put up with bullying.

## AMY'S JOURNAL

The boys arrived at our place at five.

Leo looked at me. I looked at Leo. Time stopped. It was like we were enhanced versions of ourselves, mythical and kind of impossible beings, but still us. Like we were living inside a really high-budget TV drama. Of course we looked fabulous, but this was not just a matter of impeccable grooming or confidence-boosting champagne (M & D let us have one each. And it was small.) We actually WERE fabulous. Leo was magically witty and warm. I've never felt so sparkling and funny in my life. All the way through appetizers and photos in the garden and photos with the limo, I seemed to be in a haze of sexy sparkles, floating on Leo's gaze. Each time he shot a glance at me, I soared. And okay, I floated a bit in the eyes of the other boys too, if I'm honest, and even the way the girls looked at me gave me a bit of a thrill. Because we have never looked so good or been so fun. For that first half hour in sky-high pencil-thin stiletto heels, I was walking on air. I couldn't feel the scratchy sequins of my bodice, nothing needed adjusting. I didn't even have to keep tabs on Leo or maneuver myself close to him because he was right there. Next to me. On my cloud.

Our limo arrived at the hotel in a gleaming streak of silver gorgeousness. We slid in the curvy driveway—truly this is the only moment I have ever gotten out of a limo in a curvy driveway and it was every bit as glamorous as it sounds. A guy in a suit actually opened the car door for us. Leo sprang out, extended his hand to me, and I stepped out like a princess who did this every day of her perfect life. Delicately hitched my skirt the tiniest bit, kept my knees close, toes pointed. Nailed it. The driveway was already full of other cars arriving and various parents and kids taking photos like crazy and squealing.

Did I squeal? God no. Okay, yes I did, I know I did, but I also beamed and beamed as the flashes popped all around us. This is what it's like to be a movie star. And through it all, there was Leo's hand, warm and steady whenever I reached for it, and his eyes, there for me in a way that seemed so private and connected. He seemed relaxed, he seemed to be enjoying himself, and he was looking out for me. Really. He smiled at me in the middle of this vortex of activity, as if we both KNEW that this was the start of us as US.

Then, in among all the sparkles and squeals and oh-my-gods and you-look-so-beautifuls, a figure of doom cut through the glitter like a chain saw. Sorry Ms. Kruger, you are really going to have to do something about that hair cloud of gray frizz.

"Amy, so wonderful that you're here, we just need to have a short meeting with the tech staff . . ."

Oh god, seriously?

Now?

"Of course, Ms. Kruger. Maybe later?"

"He's waiting for us now."

"In ten minutes?" (Crystal's gang was arriving! I couldn't miss this!)

"We have to give him the flash drive."

"Gabby's got the flash drive."

Leo's hand slipped from mine. In the crush of Crystal's enormous entourage of footballers, he was swept into a scrum of black shoulders. No no no! If anyone should be carried off in a sea of wide chests, sharp lapels, and crisp shirtfronts, it should be me!

"Gabby, give her the flash drive."

"I need you to go through it with him," Ms. Kruger insisted. The firm teacher voice was creeping in, which is a little unsettling to hear at the best of times and is just awful when you're in a mermaid skirt.

"I'll go," said Gabby gloomily.

"Seriously?" My eyes scanned the crowd for Leo. I couldn't afford to lose him to Macca and the gang; I might never get him back. His attention had been a lot easier to hold when there wasn't so much competition. "Would you?"

Gabby nodded.

"Thank you Gabby, you'll just have to get Amy up to speed later," said Ms. Kruger briskly in a slightly disapproving tone, but I totally didn't care. I was too busy looking for Leo, and too full of gratitude to best-friend-ever Gabby. Plus, I knew Ms. Kruger had nothing to worry about; the presentation was no problem. I can give a presentation on my head with no notice at all. I kissed Gabby thank you, and she threaded her way out of the crowd and up the sweeping carpeted staircase, following the back of Ms. Kruger's wine-colored sack dress that may well have been edgy circa 2004. We'll never know. I sprang back into the surging throng of photographers and posers, pressed my way through the footballers (which was not at all terrible), and found Leo and his magnetic hand. I was not going to let him go again tonight if I could help it.

"Leo. Amy."

A voice behind us, familiar, and yet in this context, with the soft lighting and sparkle and the scent of hair product that hung over everything like a kind of mist, I had no idea who it was. I turned around, and for a good few seconds I still had no idea. Miss Starkey? Seriously?

She's our Math teacher. She's not my favorite. I would describe her teaching style as basic. She's only been at the school for a couple of years, and I'd never seen her in anything other than her teacher's wardrobe. (She's pretty consistent: dark tailored pants and flowing blouses. Sometimes jeans. Brown hair in a ponytail, thick bangs, slash of hot lipstick. The occasional interesting shoe. She looks like a great combination of competent, businesslike, and also, weirdly, stylish and like she might tell you something funny if you ever got stuck having to talk to her. She's one of the few teachers under thirty; they do tend to stick out.) What I wasn't prepared for was the evening wear. It was one of those moments when you see teachers eating, or with their children, or basically doing anything outside of standing at the front of a classroom or telling people off for walking in the corridors at lunch. That weird glimpse of a teacher not as a teacher at all but as a person. She had her hair down, in a straight, shiny blowout, and was wearing a black wide-leg jumpsuit with a serious plunge at the front.

"Miss Starkey! I would never have recognized you!"

"I hope that's a compliment."

"Yes, you look amazing! Doesn't she look amazing, Leo?" Leo was actually looking at his phone. Ageist and rude, I thought.

"What? Oh. Sure." He barely looked up.

"Sorry Miss Starkey. He's such a boy."

"He certainly is." She half smiled, half sadly, like an outsider at a party. Which she was. For a fleeting few seconds, I actually felt sorry for her. How awful to be at anyone's school ball but your own. "Have fun," she said. "Oh—and Amy . . ." She slightly lifted her top lip and gestured toward her mouth and waved a little with one finger. The universal gesture, the code, the whisper among friends that means: you've got lipstick on your teeth. But she was not my friend, and never will be.

She drifted off into the crowd. I furiously hid my mouth with one hand and wiped at my teeth with the other as the night's first surge of hate washed over me.

**Chat: LochNess, Devinitely**
**Friday, April 14, 6 p.m.**

**LochNess:** WHERE R U?!?! I SAID DON'T BE LATE

**Group Chat: Crystal, Tallulah, Jasi, Sumaya**
**Friday, April 14, 6 p.m.**

**Tallulah:** Whoa Miss Starkey is hot?!

**Crystal:** Makes me hate her a bit less

**Jasi:** I hate her more now—Zach was practically drooling

**Sumaya:** Ugh what a pig

**Crystal:** Did you see what Ms Kruger's wearing, though?

**Sumaya:** Dress the color of a period stain

**Crystal:** Shame :/

**Tallulah:** Amy's clinging on to Leo like a mollusk

**Crystal:** In that pink dress she looks like one, too

**Jasi:** He should have asked you to the ball Crystal

**Crystal:** What makes you think he didn't

**Group Chat: Macca, Fred, Kai, Zach, Leo**
**Friday, April 14, 6 p.m.**

**Macca:** Duuuude did you see Miss Starkey?

**Kai:** I always knew she was hot

**Zach:** I'd like to square root her!

**Fred:** Shut up Zach

**Chat: Leo, 2005557764**
**Friday, April 14, 6 p.m.**

**2005557764:** Cute date

**Leo:** She's just a friend

**2005557764:** You look so hot in that suit

**Leo:** Sorry I forgot to tell you I was bringing someone

**2005557764:** What do you think of my look?

**Leo:** Stunning

**2005557764:** The outfit, or me?

**Leo:** Both

**2005557764:** Meet me upstairs

3

## Elizabeth Starkey's Statement to Police

I attended the school ball on the night of Friday, April 14, at the Pacific Crest Hotel as a supervisor. I didn't want to go and I didn't buy a ticket. I had actually planned to follow my usual routine on Fridays, which is to get takeout from Singh's in Barkerfield and watch a movie. You can check those details with the restaurant and my streaming service. Ms. Kruger, the principal, sent around an email on the Wednesday asking for more staff support at the event and I said that I would go if nobody else was available. On Thursday, Ms. Kruger came to see me in the office and asked me to be there. She said all I had to do was turn up, watch the students, and call out any bad behavior. She told me I wouldn't get paid for the night, and that it wasn't official work, but that we would get a free meal and she would be happy to approve any upcoming Personal Leave Days, and that I could leave school at lunchtime on Friday. I don't know if that's legal but other teachers were doing it so I went along with it, even though it didn't sound right to me.

I stayed at school past lunch hour to complete some grading for the Year 10s who I had first thing on Monday, so I didn't even get to leave the school until about 2:00 p.m. I then went straight home and started getting ready because Ms. Kruger wanted staff members to be at the hotel by 5:00 p.m. to supervise in case there were early arrivals, even though she told me initially that the event started at 6:00. I went home, had a quick shower, and made it to the hotel on time. There were at least 5 other staff members when I arrived, including Ms. Kruger the principal, Ben Chang the assistant principal, and Martin Kreiwoldt the Head of Health and PE. I would never drink alcohol at a school event, and it's not allowed anyway, not that that stops some people. I ordered a lemonade from the bar and stayed in the lower foyer area of the hotel to wait for the students to turn up. I didn't talk to anyone really, as Ms. Kruger, Ben, and Martin are all quite a bit older than me and we don't have much in common. I probably spent most of my time on my phone looking at social media and maybe playing a game.

As I expected, nobody arrived until at least quarter past 6. The students always have parties before the event and then they go places like Royal Park for photos so they are never early. I know this from my own experience in high school. I didn't discuss the ball with any of the students, as I don't talk to them about things like that and I only have one Year 12 class anyway. I stayed in the foyer watching everyone arrive. I can't remember who I talked to or if I talked to anyone at all. I probably said hello to the students who are in my General Math class, if I saw them, but I don't remember seeing anyone in particular.

## AMY'S JOURNAL

I felt magical. Reckless. Everything anyone said was hilariously funny, everything I said in response was devastatingly clever. Was it the champagne, or the adrenaline, or the fact that I hadn't eaten anything since breakfast? I don't know. I think it was mostly the dress. It was making a shape in the world that was more in charge of me than I was of myself. In a good way. It swept me along by Leo's side, not as just a friend or sidekick or fab colleague and classmate but as his partner. We were making history together, fulfilling roles that had been set a long time ago, like way back in the 1980s when teenage romance was invented.

We sashayed along with everyone else up the stairs to the upper foyer. Soft gold lamps lent every surface a satin sheen. Waiters in aprons fluttered around on the edges of the crowd setting up the buffet, or stalked through with trays of orange juice in champagne glasses. A professional photographer was set up with one of those paper-roll backdrops of Technicolor clouds.

I said, “Omigod! Let’s get a portrait!”

“Didn’t we do that already?”

“Oh come on, this guy has one of those silver umbrellas. It’s different!”

“They’re fifty bucks!”

“You don’t have to buy one. Just screenshot it. Look! Adorable!” I pointed to a sample photo (circa twenty years old) of a couple in the classic high school prom pose: her with a hand on hip and a wide-mouthed smile, and him standing behind, holding her waist like his life depended on it. They’re probably married with children by now.

I cleverly slid us into the queue, up against the wall, which turned out to have a delightfully tactile kind of flock wallpaper that I just had to stroke. I may have looked infantile, or sexy, it was hard to tell the difference, but it seemed that up against the wall, the lighting became even softer, the babble of the crowd became quieter, the thrilling aura even more intense. It was like we were by ourselves, or at the very least, in extreme close-up in a movie, and nobody around us mattered anymore.

Leo leaned against the wall and flicked through his phone so that the light from the screen caught tendrils of curl on his forehead and turned them into pure gold.

“I have to tell you something,” I said.

"Mmm?"

"It's a bit embarrassing."

He shrugged. "We're way past that, mate. I'm wearing eyeliner."

"Seriously?"

"No! I'm just trying to make you feel better."

"Leo!"

"Okay, I'm wearing a little bit."

I leaned in close to check. Yes, that line of lash beneath the clear green did seem even more dramatic than usual—but then so did everything else about him. He pocketed his phone and returned my gaze, as if to say: Yes you can look, yes I look amazing, and yes you may kiss me. Before I knew what was happening, my hand slid up his chest, around his neck, and my lips were on his in a moment of warm, perfect softness that stretched and stretched into a void where time seemed to stop—

And then came crashing back to reality with a sharp ding and vibration in his top pocket. Like lightning, he whipped his phone out, the kiss was over, and he was frowning at a text message and already flicking off a reply. What the actual?

"Shit. Sorry."

"Leo!"

"I gotta—"

"What?"

"Stay here."

He moved away from me and the flock wallpaper. The bubble broke and he was out there in the throng, and I could still feel him on my mouth.

Close-up over, we're back in a wide shot.

"Are you serious?" I called after him.

"No—I mean—yes, I'll get you a drink."

What the absolute freak just happened? What felt like a delightful head rush a few seconds ago now seemed to be nausea and suddenly I didn't feel quite so devastatingly brilliant. In fact, I felt abandoned, which is what I was. Our friends were mostly still downstairs, everyone else in the queue seemed a little scared of me, and I'm sure one of the waiters saw the whole thing and smirked. But what thing? What was that? It is honestly so difficult to tell the difference between a real brush-off and an accidental one.

I turned to smile my embarrassment away at the couple in the queue behind me and was relieved to see they were kissing and had probably missed the whole thing. Then they pulled their faces apart, and my relief turned to a weird mix of distaste and injury when I saw it was Bevan and that girl whose name I can never remember. She was wearing too much lace and not enough makeup.

"Oh, hi, Amy," Bevan said.

"Bevan! Isn't this great!" I smiled. (Oh, hi, says the guy who literally wrote me a love letter in the Year 12 group chat four days ago and is now publicly snogging someone else.) "You two look so great together. Love your dress, by the way." Where is Leo, why did he leave, was that a real kiss, am I in love, did he really just abandon me for a TEXT?

"Sorry, I just realized something . . ." I looked off to a fixed point somewhere else and purposefully drifted toward it. A less-than-smooth exit, but this was an emergency. I had to speak to Gabby. There are moments like this when only your best friend will do.

**Group Chat: Crystal, Tallulah, Jasi, Sumaya**
**Friday, April 14, 6:30 p.m.**

**Tallulah:** Yikes—looks like Amy was a pity date. Just saw them kiss and he practically sprinted away.

**Crystal:** Who's surprised?

**Sumaya:** Ugh now she's gonna weep all through her presentation

## Chris Butt's Incident Report

I started work as usual and I was just at my desk setting up for the night and then the lady who I think was the principal came up and asked me if everything was OK for the presentation and I had to say what do you mean and she said you know, the presentation, and I didn't know anything about any presentation. There was nothing about it on the system and I showed her that but she said there was definitely a presentation with music and a slideshow even though those should always be listed in the system as per the procedure and there was nothing there.

She came up a bit later with a girl who had a flash drive and then she just said make it work and left. That's definitely not procedure but it's not the first time I've had to clear up other people's mess. The girl told me that the presentation was just pictures of the school and a song and we plugged it in and I had a quick look and it seemed fine. I don't know if they had approval but I hooked it up, and that's an issue for a private hirer not our problem. She wanted the screen up and I couldn't leave the desk because security so she got the screen out and put it up at her own risk. That was when the other girl in the pink dress came in so it's possible that's why she didn't do it properly but I wouldn't know as that wasn't my call. She decided to do it on her own, nothing to do with me.

## AMY'S JOURNAL

I somehow found my way to the ballroom, which was deserted, apart from Gabby up on the stage, a tech dude in a black

T-shirt and jeans at the tech desk, and a few hundred gold and black balloons. Careful, don't slip on the parquet flooring. Stilettos are not made for running, or walking quickly, or indeed walking at all, come to think of it. I tippy-toed up to Gabby as fast as I could, where she was having some kind of fight on the stage with a display screen. The tech dude was too far away to hear our conversation, not that it really mattered. He looked like the kind of guy who never really pays attention to what you say, even when you say it right to his face.

I poured out my sorry story to Gabby, and as I retold it, suddenly it didn't seem quite so sorry after all. Perhaps I had been distracted by the Bevan factor—his presence seemed to highlight the abandonment aspect, but when I thought about it, what stuck out most clearly was the moment of the kiss.

"Did he kiss you back?"

"Well—yes."

"And then he ran off?"

"Like, sprinted."

"That's not good."

"But he did kiss me back."

"Hm."

"That means he likes me, right?"

Gabby was struggling too much with the screen to reply. These things should be designed better.

"Right?" I said again.

"Hey, careful with that," yelled T-shirt guy from the sound desk.

"Ow." I think the top of the screen hit her on the head. She really wasn't concentrating.

"You don't kiss a girl like that if you don't like her," I insisted. It was becoming very clear to me what had happened. This was a world-changing kiss. A seismic shift in the course of the night—and indeed our lives. This was The Moment. Leo was as much taken by surprise as I was. Macca or one of those other goons texted him and he reacted like that because he was actually in shock.

"I don't even know why I'm second-guessing myself like this. I must be crazy. Thanks babe, you're the best."

I had to find him again, look into his eyes again, and kiss him again. Just to make sure.

---

***Transcription of Detective Wozniak's interview with Leo Prince***

**SW:** I must inform you that this interview is being recorded. I must inform you that you do not have to say or do anything, but anything you say or do may be given as evidence in court. Do you understand?

**LEO:** Yes.

**SW:** Do you agree to proceed with the interview?

**LEO:** Yes.

**SW:** Can you please state your name for the recording?

**LEO:** Leo.

**SW:** Your full name?

**LEO:** Is this going to take long?

**SW:** If you don't mind?

**LEO:** 'Cause I've got a–

**SW:** Not long.

**LEO:** –thing . . . meeting up–

**SW:** Your dad said he'd drive you. We've got a good 40 minutes.

**LEO:** And I gotta get ready.

**SW:** Until 5. According to your dad.

*(pause)*

**LEO:** What do you want to know?

**SW:** Just . . . your name.

**LEO:** Leonard Roger Prince.

**SW:** Great, so as I told you and your dad, we're just getting a bit of an idea about what happened the other night at the ball. We've talked to a few people and we want to get a clearer picture.

**LEO:** I don't know anything.

**SW:** You were there though.

**LEO:** Everyone was there.

**SW:** People have told us–

**LEO:** It was kind of a public event.

**SW:** –some things, but there's a bit we're trying to piece together here.

**LEO:** I really don't know what I can tell you.

**SW:** Specifically about you and one of the staff.

**LEO:** Yeah well . . . I mean, there's nothing much to say about that is there. I think everyone saw what happened, so.

**SW:** What happened?

**LEO:** I got in trouble, got yelled at. I mean, if you're going to interview everyone who gets yelled at by a teacher . . .

**SW:** We're really just interested in what you have to say.

**LEO:** I don't have anything to say.

*(pause)*

**SW:** Right.

**LEO:** Look, I'm sorry you had to come out here and everything but–

**SW:** Where were you earlier on in the night?

**LEO:** What?

**SW:** Some of your friends said there was about an hour where you were missing.

**LEO:** Who said that?

**SW:** Nobody saw you.

**LEO:** Who?

**SW:** A few people.

**LEO:** Well that's bullshit.

**SW:** You were at the ball the whole time, then?

**LEO:** Yeah. I arrived with everyone else, there's photos, there's like a shitload of them, did you even look?

*(pause)*

**LEO:** Sorry, I'm just a bit . . . on edge. You know.

**SW:** My understanding is that you and your friends arrived together, and you were in the lower foyer with everyone else for about 10 minutes, and then you went up the stairs, with your partner . . . um . . .

**LEO:** Amy.

**SW:** With Amy. And then people saw the two of you lining up for a photo, for a portrait, but there was no portrait taken. And that's the last anyone saw of you. For quite a while.

*(pause)*

**SW:** Do you mind telling me what happened?

*(pause)*

**LEO:** The thing is, it's not just about me.

**SW:** This is a confidential conversation.

**LEO:** It's kind of personal and . . . awkward. For other people, I mean.

**SW:** What other people, Leo?

**LEO:** I don't want to embarrass anyone.

**SW:** I can talk to Amy directly.

**LEO:** No.

**SW:** No?

**LEO:** I mean, that's a bit unnecessary. Isn't it?

**SW:** But if she's a part of this–

**LEO:** But I don't know if she'd tell you the truth, you know what I mean?

**SW:** What is the truth?

**LEO:** I mean, she could make shit up.

**SW:** Why would she do that?

*(pause)*

**LEO:** Look, you've got it on tape and everything, that I didn't want to go into this. As far as I'm concerned it's private, it's between me and Amy, but if you're going to talk to her, then I've just got to say, she really . . . she might . . . not . . . um . . . she might not be truthful. Because the absolute truth is, she had a bit of an embarrassing night. In more ways than one.

**SW:** I'm really just interested in you telling me what happened to you.

4

## ✉ Gabby Gibson's Email to the Principal—Page 1

Hi Ms. Kruger,

I'm really sorry about Friday night. My dad made me write this, but I want you to know I would of done it anyway. I know your busy but I have to explain what happened and how things turned out the way they did. It wasn't because of anyone at the hotel, even though the tech guy was a bit weird. It was kind of my fault but it was really all just an accident and a misunderstanding and I wish it never happened.

At the start of the night I had the flash drive in my clutch because Amy's evening purse was very small and she couldn't fit anything much in it and also it's a bit see-through (very fine chain mail, I also had her tampons just in case). So I wasn't really in charge of the slideshow presentation thing at all really. I was just like an extra handbag. Then when you came and asked Amy to set it all up at the start of the night, it wasn't really my job at all, only Amy didn't want to do it. She was super into Leo, if you know what I mean, and when we got to the ball she was really happy and just wanted to be with him and I would just have been hanging around being a third wheel anyway, so I went up with you to the ballroom to do the presentation.

Then when we got there as you know the guy was a bit of a pain because he didn't know there was a presentation at all, and then when you left he got even worse and said things like "not my problem" and "I didn't have the paperwork." But he said he could do it as long as I set it up right and it all went fine although I broke a nail setting up the screen. I didn't know how it worked and the guy said he couldn't leave the sound desk because of security concerns. So I did it and it was harder than it looks, I don't know if I did it right, but the tech guy said it was fine and I trusted him.

## AMY'S JOURNAL

I left Gabby and the T-shirt guy and tippy-toed back out into the upper foyer area where the buffet was almost ready. All the stragglers were there—everyone was there—and it was a bit of a struggle to get through all those compliments.

"You look amazing! Is that a Victor Drummoyne? Did you do your own hair? How much were those shoes?"

"Thank you! Yes it is. Of course I did. I'm not telling you that! And have you seen Leo anywhere?"

I must have done a full lap and a half before I spotted the corridor on the other side of the elevators, where Hyun Jae was loitering, looking lost while Miss Starkey berated her for being somewhere off-limits. Right. I slipped past them and found open double doors to an empty conference room, with stacks of chairs around the walls, and Leo skulking in the middle, face still buried in his phone.

"Leo!"

"Hey. Sorry." He pocketed his phone, a little sheepishly.

"What's going on?"

"It was my parents. Let's go get some—" He took my hand as he moved toward the door, but I caught him and drew him close. I was fast, more definite. This wasn't going to be another off-guard rush of romance. I was going to make this moment happen.

I pulled his face toward mine, but our lips barely touched. He turned his cheek, blocked my arm, and resisted. Not just resisted—pushed. Unmistakably. What? My whole body jolted and my stomach fell, like I'd trodden on a stair that wasn't there.

"Sorry."

Blood rushed to my cheeks, hot water to my eyes. Not sad tears, but hot liquid rage.

"Sorry?"

"Can't we just go—" He gestured desperately toward the door. He seemed genuinely distressed. "Come on. Don't make this weird."

"You pushed me!"

"I was just mucking around."

"You're my date."

His eyes flashed with suspicion. "What's that supposed to mean? We're not going out."

"We are going out. This is out."

"You know what I mean."

"This is our school ball, Leo. You don't go to the ball with just anyone; you go with someone important, someone—" Someone you like. But I couldn't bring myself to say that. "It's supposed to mean something. It does mean something."

My words hung in the air between us, and I wanted to go back to ten minutes ago, to sparkly Amy, happy Amy. Had I ruined everything? Was it all my fault? But I could still feel the pressure on my arms where he pushed me, like a burn. You don't do that, and he knew it. Whether he liked me or didn't like me or whatever, you don't go to the ball with someone and then physically push them away. He couldn't meet my eyes.

*Ding*—his phone went off again and his hand whipped up

to check it. Reflex action. Seriously? And then the horrible truth dawned on me.

"Are you seeing someone else?"

"No."

"Who's that from then?"

"No one. My dad."

I lunged for the phone. He deflected and held it out of my reach, which was way too easy for someone six feet tall in a suit to do to someone else who is totally nowhere near that and unable to jump, bend, lunge, or indeed walk properly. It was all so silly that I actually started to giggle, in a kind of crying sort of a way.

"Give it!"

"No!"

"GIVE IT!" I scrambled, he fended me off, and his hands touched my ribs, up to the skin under my arms, in a play fight that I almost started enjoying.

"All right, all right." It's all fun and games until—"I am seeing someone. Happy now?"—someone loses an eye.

I lost an eye.

The building hysteria faded into a pathetic numbness.

"Are you serious right now?"

His phone dinged in his pocket again, as if to mock me. Right. It's her. Dinging away, ever since the start of the night. Our night together. My night.

"Who is it?"

He looked down, toward the door, anywhere but at me.

"Who is it, Leo?"

"It's kind of a secret."

"Is she here?"

He nodded.

Oh my freaking god. Why don't you just stab me in the heart and be done with me. I thought I had him, that I was closer to Leo than I'd ever been, but he was never even there. He was off in a cozy partnership with someone else, someone who was not me. I was worse than dateless. I was Not Good Enough.

"But you're still my date. For the night," he scrambled defensively as I squirmed away from his touch. "No one has to know. We can still—you know . . ." His voice died out into nothing. He didn't dare say it.

"What? Pretend?" It was all becoming horribly clear. "You need me to cover for you?"

This whole time, my bliss was just a charade. I was a puppet in some elaborate performance to divert attention away from the fact that he's actually with someone else entirely. The dizzying whirl of the ball and everything leading up to it was just a sham. And the worst thing is, I'm already committed, manipulated into the deepest part of the show, acting it out, in the most humiliating way possible. Unawares. He doesn't want to be with me, he doesn't want me at all, and he never did.

"No! I'm just trying to do the right thing." I could almost believe him, except obviously he didn't give a flying whatever about my feelings.

"Don't touch me." I shoved his hand away and stalked to the door. "You dick."

I held myself together for as long as I could as I stalked off, back to the party that I no longer wanted to be a part of. The carpet blurred through bubbling tears, the romantic lighting just looked sickly, the buzzing crowd was strange—immature and loud. The mood had become more boisterous, but people had found their cliques so I was able to slip through relatively unnoticed, face plastered with an irrationally frozen smile. *Hi. Yeah great. Absolutely.* I made a beeline for the ballroom, but that was starting to fill up now too as people wandered around memorizing the seating plan and admiring those stupid balloons. I couldn't stop now, I had to keep going, in a straight line, straight for those glass doors on the opposite wall, and I wished to god I could crash right through them and emerge into tomorrow. Or better yet, yesterday.

## Elizabeth Starkey's Statement to Police

When the ballroom opened at around 7:00 I went upstairs and found my seat at the teachers' table. There were probably some people in the room at that point, I don't really remember. I wasn't feeling well. I actually got my period and I suffer from quite bad cramps. It's always been that way for me. My department head Madeleine Morris knows as it sometimes gets so bad that I can't work, even though I try to push through it. One time last year she came into my classroom and I was trying to teach through the pain, but she could tell I wasn't okay and she made me leave the room and go lie down. I always have the strongest possible painkillers in my bag, and in my desk at work, and in my car. All my friends and family know this about me, you can ask anyone, as well as my doctor, if you want proof. So when this happened at the ball, I decided the best thing to do would be just to have a bit of a walk in the fresh air. I didn't want to bother anyone with it.

I left my handbag at my place on the table. I did this because I didn't think I'd be gone long and it was a clutch purse that's actually quite inconvenient to hold. It is rectangular and black with two rows of rhinestones. It's quite distinctive, in fact two of the Year 12 girls had already commented on it so I'm sure that people would have seen it on the table and known it was mine. I left it there and went outside. I didn't tell anyone and I didn't encounter anyone. I just walked around in the park area close to the hotel down toward the river. I must have been there for around an hour.

## *Transcription of Detective Wozniak's interview with Leo Prince*

**LEO:** Okay, I'll tell you what happened. Amy, she . . . um . . . came on to me, okay? Like, had a crush on me, or whatever. And when we were in the line for that photo, she tried to kiss me. Okay? So, now you know.

**SW:** And what did you do?

**LEO:** Look, it was bad, okay?

**SW:** You don't like her?

**LEO:** She is a great girl. She's, like, really funny and super smart and we get on. Like, really get on, you know, like friends, but, yeah. I didn't know she felt that way, to be honest.

**SW:** So what did you do?

**LEO:** I . . . um. Well. I . . . geez. This is not nice. You know. I don't like talking about it. I feel bad.

**SW:** Why?

**LEO:** Because . . . I didn't want to disappoint her. She put a lot of effort into the night.

**SW:** Did you tell her you didn't like her?

**LEO:** No! I mean, I do like her. She was my date.

**SW:** So what did you say?

**LEO:** I . . . um. I told her I was seeing someone else.

**SW:** Who?

**LEO:** Nobody.

**SW:** You didn't tell her who?

**LEO:** No . . . 'cause . . . it wasn't actually true.

**SW:** Really?

**LEO:** No, it was all a lie. I didn't mean it. I mean, that's what you do, right, when someone is interested in you and you're not interested in them, you say, oh, I've got a boyfriend, I've got a girlfriend, whatever, it's just a nice way of letting people down. I think.

**SW:** So—what happened then?

**LEO:** Well. She was still upset. And she went off . . . and whatever, I can't really talk about what happened to her. That's her business.

## AMY'S JOURNAL

I shoved my way straight out the long wall of glass doors into a pretty little garden terrace, with square stones, a view over the open park down to the river, white marble planters, and a maze of bushes cut into neat shapes, sprinkled with fairy lights. But I barely took in any of it, as my humiliation felt too complete. The Victor Drummoyne I had felt so proud of now felt like a sick joke, like I didn't deserve to wear it. Truly. All that time and money wasted.

"Amy?"

Gabby appeared behind me. At the first sound of softness and sympathy, I totally crumbled in an unholy heap of sobs.

"He's seeing someone else!" I collapsed into her arms.

"Yeah."

"What? You knew?"

She shrugged. "He's a good-looking guy. That's what they do." She gently wiped away the mascara smudges. "At least now you know."

My face exploded in a fresh bout of snotty sobs. "But that doesn't stop me from liking him!"

Gabby leaned on the railing and smiled, like you would at a little kid crying over not being allowed to have something ridiculous, like pink light-up shoes. But Leo is not pink light-up shoes. He is actually, legitimately beautiful. And an asshole.

"Don't smile!" I hiccupped.

"I'm not smiling!"

"It's not funny!"

"I know, it's devastating!"

"I'm devastated."

*Snap*. Gabby whipped out her phone and took a photo of me being totally devastated.

"Don't!" My makeup was wrecked, I was sweating. Snot was pooling on my upper lip.

"You look incredible."

I checked out the shot as I wiped snot away with the back of my hand and it was actually true. The sky behind me was a magnificent shade of purple, the skyscrapers were speckled with yellow lights, the fairy lights everywhere gave off a luminosity that looked professionally designed. Turns out tear-smudged smoky eye is still pretty smoky, gently kissed lipstick is still satin, and crying is great for heightening color and brightening eyes. It was going to take more than a few minutes of total disaster to completely ruin several months' worth of grooming after all, and actually maybe a little emotional upheaval was just what I needed to give me an edge.

"Take another one." So she took another one. And another one, and another one. Full length, up close, mid-shot, we did all of them and I was a tearfully enthusiastic supermodel. Each artsy setup made me feel just a little more validated and a little less like absolute trash.

"Here, pick your favorite," Gabby said as she thrust her phone at me. I flicked through them—so many already. It seems it really is possible to create more than one completely different pose per second. It wasn't until I had flicked through all of them and selected five of the absolute best that I noticed what Gabby was doing. Around behind one of the square planters, she was actually squatting down and—okay, there is no elegant way of saying this—peeing. Like, for real. Totally in vintage emerald green, between a box planter and a balustrade, in the middle of the city, in the most magnificent lighting ever.

"Oh my god Gabby!"

"What?"

"Seriously?"

"I had to go!"

"Those are glass doors!"

"No one can see me." It's true, she was in a kind of protected cubbyhole between planters and the balcony wall, but still the glass doors to the ballroom went the whole length of the terrace. "It's dark out here anyway." While we could clearly see the gathering crowds milling about the tables inside, all they could probably see were their own reflections and maybe a shadow or two of the fairy-lit planters.

"You look so trashy!" I laughed. She mimed picking her nose with a perfectly manicured hand. *Snap!* Well who wouldn't? We both fell about in giggles. She did a little dry-off shake and I couldn't help it, I was overcome with hysterical laughter and—oh no, thanks a lot, Gabby! "Now I've got to go too!" I tippy-toed over and gave her the phone, and within seconds shimmied my undies right off and my skirt all the way up to my waist. Trust me, there was no other way of doing this. That mermaid skirt fit like skin, my undies were just lacy elastic bands, and in shoes and my state of mixed devastation, euphoria, and hysteria, I didn't trust my aim. Gabby doubled over in fits of laughter, of course.

"What are you doing?" Easy for her to say, she had a circle skirt.

"It cost eight hundred bucks. I'm not going to pee on it!"

Gabby lined up to take a photo.

"Don't you dare!"

"But you look so lovely!"

"Gabby . . ." It's difficult to sound threatening when you're still laughing and trying to pee straight. "Don't!" She walked off and let me finish, thank goodness, because the only thing less elegant than yanking your undies down and your skirt up is trying to wrench them back again.

"Let me see."

"Hang on!" She tapped a few more keys on her phone. Very funny, pretending to post.

"I am deleting those right now! Give it here!"

She smiled cheekily and handed the phone over.

"What did you do?"

"Nothing." More cheeky grinning.

"What?"

"Nothing!"

"You didn't post that. Oh no Gabby you didn't."

I grabbed the phone. Oh god. Hair, piss, undies, cellulite. It's all I could see. And she'd forwarded it to our friendship chat group.

"Oh my freaking god."

"Ha! You are a total queen, my friend!" Like this was a picture of me in a tiara.

I stared at her in total incomprehension.

"That's how much fun you're having," she giggled. "Who needs a date!"

"Are you psychotic? Are you on drugs?"

"It's only a joke."

"You sent it."

"To our friends. They won't show anyone. You can't see anything anyway—" She flinched backward as I nearly punched the screen into her face. She took the phone and squinted over it (to be fair, she is super nearsighted). She paused and considered, and her stupid smile melted right off, as it should, and was replaced by a look of slight panic. Which was nothing compared to the super panic I was experiencing.

"Oh. God. That's kind of bad." It's the moment of diagnosis, the moment when things haven't turned to shit quite yet but you know it's definitely going to happen and it's going to happen SOON.

**Group Chat: Amy, Gabby, Kate, Bianca, Veronika**
**Friday, April 14, 7 p.m.**

**Kate:** OMG AMY! I think this should be ur yearbook photo?

5

SCHOOL COMMUNITY NEWSLETTER

## FROM THE PRINCIPAL'S DESK

Behavior at the event was not of the exemplary type that we as a school have come to expect from our students when in public. This is completely unrelated to any of the other incidents, as before there was any indication of anything going wrong, I observed several students behaving raucously. This included swearing, a little rough play inappropriate to a formal event, and also some of the balloons on the table centerpieces were deliberately popped. This was of great disappointment to me personally, as I know the School Ball Fundraising and Decorating Committee put a great deal of thought and effort into choosing the centerpieces, transporting them to the venue, and arranging them. They were quite clearly not for touching, they were for being looked at. I made an announcement to this effect some time before the dinner proceedings, well before anything untoward happened. It is quite possible that for these reasons alone, the decision would already have been made to hold next year's school ball on school property in the school gym. I realize the Year Elevens are bearing the brunt of the consequences for what has happened, which is unfortunate because it wasn't their fault. However, it is essential for us to draw clear boundaries, and the Year Twelves might like to think seriously about how their behavior has affected others.

### ✉ Gabby Gibson's Email to the Principal—Page 2

So then later Amy came into the ballroom and she was super upset so we went out on the balcony. We started taking photos of each other. We didn't mean them to be rude or anything. It's just that I needed to go and I don't know if you know but the bathrooms were a really long way away from the balcony and there's always a line and girls in there doing makeup and stuff and I just thought it would be quicker and easier to just pee behind a bush. Which is what we do in our family when we go on car trips and things because it really is a lot quicker and easier and plus I have three brothers. So I did it first and then Amy had to go too and then I truly was just being silly and trying to cheer her up by taking funny photos. It would have been really funny except that I didn't know you could actually see her private parts.

"Oh no."

On the other side of the glass doors, I could see Kate and Bianca gaping over a phone, eyes wide, delighting in the drama. And I saw them shoot a swift glance around the room, target Crystal and her gang of strapless and bodycon dresses. I saw them revel in the taboo, taste the scandal, and press send. I saw the very moment Crystal's phone went *ding*, and I saw her reach for her phone. The picture hit Crystal with the force of a body blow. I heard her squeal through the double glazing. She was instantly surrounded by a crush of carefully waved heads. Then she sent it on. Another little giggling group sprouted—then another—then a bigger group. Our entire cohort gradually became aware something outrageous was happening. Then it hit the footballers, who roared. I watched with horror as the virus spread in real time: the virus of Amy Middleton's vagina. Phones lit up all over the ballroom, first sporadically, then faster, in clusters, then all at once. People ran, they crowded, they snickered, they posted, they captioned, they made memes, and I watched it all in panoramic view as though it was happening in slow motion. My own private horror film.

"Oh my freaking god."

"It's just a stupid photo. It's nothing," squeaked Gabby, fully aware that this photo was not stupid, nor would it ever, ever be nothing.

"My life is over!"

"It was just meant to be fun!"

Fun? This was anything but fun. For the second time that night I actually felt like a movie star, but this time in the violated way, and it was not good.

"You posted porn!"

"No I didn't—"

"Of me! On purpose!"

"I didn't know that you could see—"

"My undies were off! What did you expect?"

"Well you started it!"

"You started it! I didn't even need to go!"

"I'm sorry, okay?" She was nearly in tears.

"So? How does that help? This is me now, forever. Piss, thighs, cellulite, enormous vagina. In a Victor Drummoyne!"

"I honestly didn't mean—"

"Oh bullshit, Gabby."

"I didn't!"

"This isn't an accident, this is a hate crime."

"What?"

"I'm pretty, and smart, and popular, and you're a fucking jealous bitch. Well congratulations, you win." I whipped off my stilettos, scraped my ridiculous mermaid skirt up to my knees, and turned my back on her. "I'm out!" I shouted as I strode away into the dark.

Thank goodness I found a set of steps leading down from the terrace to the lawn below. Nothing worse than storming off and having to storm back again, although I was so mad at that point that if I had to, I could have borne it.

"Amy!" she called out after me.

"I hate you!" I spat back, and disappeared into a maze of unlit landscape architecture. All I wanted to do was put as much distance between me and that terrace and the rest of my life as I possibly could.

Within minutes, I was far enough away to turn back and see Gabby, a forlorn figure silhouetted against the sky, leaning over the terrace railing. "Amy!" she called. But she was just a disconnected shriek on the wind, part of another world that I was never, ever going to be part of again.

"Fuck you!" I screeched back. First time I've ever said that to someone. I'm not going to lie, it felt fucking fantastic. She slumped, turned away, and slunk back toward the pumping music. Swallowed up by the glittering golden glow of a party with pretty much all the people I knew in the world, who had now all seen me squatting mid-piss.

### ✉ Gabby Gibson's Email to the Principal—Page 3

Amy was really upset when she found out and so was I. She got very mad at me to be honest and yelled at me even though I was just joking around and didn't mean it to be bad. She stormed away into the dark and left me there and then I didn't even have anyone to sit with or hang out with and I felt terrible. I didn't even want to have fun, and Kate and Bianca, who are supposed to be our friends, they were no help at all. They said they didn't forward the pic to anyone but I know they did because by the time I got into the ballroom everyone was snickering and kind of looking at me strange, and then when I sat down Kate and Bianca came up and pretended to be like all caring but really they were just enjoying the scandal of it and everything. I don't think I'm going to hang out with them anymore to be honest. Anyway I'm not trying to throw them under the bus but you should know I only posted the pic in our group, which is Kate, Bianca, Amy, and me and I think Veronika who left halfway through Year 11. She might still be on it but she's at Sacred Hart now and never posts anything.

**Group Chat: Crystal, Tallulah, Jasi, Sumaya**
**Friday, April 14, 7 p.m.**

**Tallulah:** OMG

**Jasi:** Holy shit!

**Crystal:** Pride of Anderson High falls from grace

**Sumaya:** Has Leo seen it?

**Jasi:** Dunno

**Crystal:** Someone should send it to him

**Jasi:** He'll probably dump her :(

**Crystal:** They're not together genius

**Jasi:** I kind of feel sorry for her

**Crystal:** She brought it on herself—u wouldn't catch me peeing in a bush in Victor Drummoyne

**Group Chat: Macca, Kai, Fred, Zach, Leo**
**Friday, April 14, 7 p.m.**

**Fred:** Whoa check this out

**Kai:** You can see everything

**Macca:** Smash or pass?

**Zach:** Pass. Ruined the mystery.

## ***Transcription of Detective Wozniak's interview with Leo Prince***

**SW:** So Amy told you that she liked you, and then she left you in an empty function room away from the main party. What did you do then?

**LEO:** I . . . um. I was feeling pretty shit actually.

**SW:** Because of what she said.

**LEO:** Yeah.

**SW:** So what did you do? Where did you go?

**LEO:** And the whole ball thing was just pissing me off. Sorry, can I swear?

**SW:** If that makes it easier.

**LEO:** It was just kind of fucked up, you know? The whole thing. Amy and all the other girls all dressed up like fucking Real Housewives, all the guys in these dumb rented suits. I mean, we're kids, right? We haven't even graduated from school yet, half of us aren't allowed to drink or vote or anything, and we're in a fucking ballroom. Like this is supposed to be meaningful. It's ludicrous. I was just going along with it, but when Amy got salty, I don't know, I just felt like shit.

**SW:** So what did you do?

**LEO:** I don't want to say.

*(pause)*

**LEO:** Okay. I'm going to tell you. And I'm not proud of it, and it doesn't make me look good, but it's actually the truth. Whatever anyone else says, okay?

**SW:** Okay.

**LEO:** I . . . I stole a teacher's keys. Miss Starkey. I took her keys, and . . . I took her car out. For a spin.

**SW:** Really.

**LEO:** Yeah. I know, it's bad. I haven't told anyone. Dad doesn't know either and I'm going to get into a shit-load of trouble for this, but it is what it is. I was just so pissed off, I thought I'd, you know, hightail it out of there.

**SW:** How did you get her keys?

**LEO:** I . . . snuck into the ballroom, didn't talk to any-one, nobody talked to me, I guess nobody saw me. I didn't plan it or anything of course. I just saw her bag there and her keys kind of hanging out of it and I thought, fuck it. I'm outta here.

**SW:** You knew her bag?

**LEO:** I saw her holding it before. And her keys, I knew her keys, 'cause she's got this dumb fluffy keyring thing and it's always on her desk in the classroom, everyone knows that. And everyone knows which cars the teachers all drive; at high school it's like the first thing you learn.

**SW:** How did you know she drove to the ball? Or where she parked?

**LEO:** Took a gamble. Found the car in the parking lot. I was right. So.

**SW:** And then you drove it.

**LEO:** Yeah. And . . . this is kind of shit, but I mean, you asked for it, so here goes . . . I was driving a bit fast, like, faster than I should have, and I was heading down that road that goes through the park toward the river, and . . . um . . . I just . . . wasn't paying attention and I hit something. On the road. I hit the goat.

**SW:** The what?

**LEO:** The goat. I hit it. With Miss Starkey's car.

**SW:** You hit a goat? In the middle of the city?

**LEO:** It was in the middle of that big-ass park, but yeah. I hit the goat. It was me.

**SW:** Why was there a goat?

**LEO:** They didn't tell you about the goat?

**SW:** No.

**LEO:** Well. Then you have pretty much missed the point of the whole fucking night.

## AMY'S JOURNAL

I stormed off into the dark, not caring where I was going. Into nothingness, vaguely aware of the hotel and the city receding behind me, the empty playing fields in front of me, and the distant road along the river beyond. It was all shadows and empty air, the kind of place that gives girls everywhere the absolute chills, and all I wanted was for it to swallow me up. Better to throw myself into the hands of park-dwelling rapists and murderers than to face anyone I knew ever again.

I was too angry to be frightened. Come and get me, criminals, I dare you. I'll smash these stilettos in your faces and freaking enjoy it. But as I walked, the outrage drained away and left nothing but despair. I couldn't fight off an attacker. I could barely walk; I was barefoot, treading on prickles, holding my shoes and my skirt, still hobbled by my dress binding me at the knees. Where was I going? I couldn't just keep walking indefinitely, on a straight line through nothing to nowhere. Something has to give, something has to happen. Could I possibly get struck by lightning? Please? How likely is that? Does lightning just come out of the blue? It must. There must be that first strike that nobody is expecting. And it could hit me, and nobody would know until morning, and what would M & D say when they found out that an amateur football team at Saturday practice discovered me dead by electrocution? In my $800 dress? Or would the lightning burn it all off? And which picture would they put on the news? God, not a school photo. Please. I really must tell them which photo to use in case of disaster.

As these thoughts swirled around in my head, a scene gradually came into focus. Ahead of me, a row of streetlights cut straight through the park, across my line of vision. It's a road, one of those connecting streets that's hardly used joining the back-end mess of the city with the main road along the river. And looming somewhere on the edges of the pools of light were three figures—all shadowy, all in black—and one of them . . . on all fours? Running? Skittering and bouncing? Surely that's too big to be a dog? And I could hear people shouting and I saw this animal do a playful little hop straight into the road, into full light—and it was a cute horned brown-and-white goat! What? Surely not. I blinked in surprise. But yes, that's what it was, and it was being stalked by these two figures on the other side of the road, who were still half in darkness, but seemed to be calling to it. Before I could make sense of this bizarre scene, I heard the swoosh of a descending car. It approached at speed, down the hill from the city, and nobody seemed to know it was coming, not even me, and then *BANG*, it plowed straight into the goat, sent it flying through the air, over the top of the car, and it landed with a horrible smack on the center white line. The car screeched to a stop. A white car. Before I knew it, I was running, stupid high heels clattering in my hand, my boobs rubbed raw by netting and all the sequin sewing on the inside of the top, little pink nipple covers long since migrated to my waist, and I was standing over this bleeding, mangled mess of fur and horn and limbs with two strangers.

"Oh my god!"

The three of us stood there, me panting, the other two just staring in shocked silence. The car idled askew on the road a couple of hundred meters away—then *VRRRRM*—it sped away to the main road and disappeared into the distant snake of traffic, toward the entrance to the freeway.

---

***Transcription of Detective Wozniak's interview with Leo Prince***

**SW:** What happened next?

**LEO:** Well I hit something on the road, didn't I.

**SW:** What did you do?

*(pause)*

**SW:** Leo? Did you stop the car, did you go back to help? Leo?

**LEO:** *(inaudible)*

**SW:** Pardon?

**LEO:** No.

**SW:** You—just—

**LEO:** I didn't go back, okay? I . . . I was scared. I saw that it wasn't a person or anything, I could see everyone there was okay, out the back window. So I just drove off. I kept going.

**SW:** You drove off?

**LEO:** I know it was wrong. I knew it then. And I changed my mind pretty quick. I turned around, I took the car back, and I found them.

## AMY'S JOURNAL

As the car revved away, someone yelled after it, "Fucking animals!" I looked up in surprise. This wasn't a stranger. I knew this guy. I knew both of them. From English Literature. They sit in the back, looking superior. The only time they open their mouths is to decry something as sexist, racist, classist, homophobic, ableist, or all five, or just bad. Worst thing is, they're usually right. She's kind of goth, he's kind of weird.

"It's you!"

At school they have a uniform of gray angry sloppiness so

I was a bit shocked to see him in a full-on vintage navy-blue velvet-trimmed suit with a pale pink shirt with a front ruffle and a velvet bow tie. That kind of outfit takes either a lot of preparation, or (as I suspect was the case here) a very stylish grandparent who really took care of his old stuff. She was in a black tunic, leggings, and boots. And piercings. And a bad mood.

"Are you wearing that to the ball?" I asked.

"What? No!"

Vanessa. That's her name.

She just kept staring down at the goat.

"Where did it come from?" I asked.

Vanessa and her friend just shrugged and stared.

Oh god, it was so awful. I didn't want to look—I don't think any of us wanted to look—but we couldn't help it. It was so pathetic there in the middle of the road, silent and immobile, just fur and blood and shallow yellow eyes, all distant in the light.

"Maaaa!"

All three of us leaped back in horror.

"Oh my god! It's still alive!"

The boy disappeared into the edges of the darkness, breathing hard, doubled over with his hands on his hips.

"What are we going to do?" I asked.

"How should I know?" spat Vanessa.

The goat exploded out of its apparent coma. It struggled and panted, as if it was trying to get up.

"We have to do something! It's in pain!" I begged.

"It's not our fault!"

"We should call someone."

"No!" they both shouted at the same time, a little too fast.

"I mean, why?" Vanessa added, a little more calmly, but still belligerent. "There's nothing anyone can do."

We stared down at it. Its breath came in short, rattly gasps. Blood pooled out behind it, coming from god knows where, while ripped skin around its stomach and legs gaped shiny and pink.

"Well let's get it off the road at least!"

I moved toward it, but Vanessa, on the other side of the road, just stood staring and the other guy hovered behind her, barely a smudge in the dark.

"Guys? She might cause another accident!"

"I'm not touching it."

I'm no crazy animal-lover. I'm not vegan. I'm not even vegetarian. If I see a cockroach, I will kill it dead by whatever means possible. But there was something about this goat that reminded me of myself. We'd both been smashed and left to die. It was all a terrible disaster, no matter which way you looked at it, but there was no way I was going to let this goat suffer alone.

I looked up and down the road—nothing coming. No sound but the rattly, gaspy heaving of this poor animal at our feet.

I swept my hair back, hitched up my skirt, dropped my shoes on the curb, and stepped out into the light. The goat's breathing seemed to get louder, and I could smell it now too—a salty, tangy, animal-poo kind of smell that came off the poor thing in a fog of heat. Oh dear. I instinctively arched my face away as I bent down over it, and held my breath as I reached my arms underneath, into the warmth of fur and something wet, and the rasp of the asphalt, and oh my god, I'm going to be sick. But then I heard the heaving, retching sounds of the boy somewhere off in the darkness and that just galvanized me somehow. This poor creature needed our help; this was no time to collapse. At first I tried to scoop it up and hold it just with my forearms, and keep the fur and the smell and everything away from my dress, but it was heavier than I thought, and all torn and incomplete. Its limbs and neck all draped away and I had to clutch the whole thing to my chest so I wouldn't drop it or fall over. And it felt strangely comforting, like I was hugging it, but as I lurched to my feet, one of my tulle underskirt frills must have slipped down and I put one foot right through it, which jerked me straight down onto my knees.

"Ow!"

"Quick! There's a car!"

I could hear it too. The lights glanced off me, and the goat. I scrambled to no avail, I was stuck. My knees were stinging, I couldn't let go, I couldn't haul myself up. Next thing I knew, Vanessa was next to me, her cool narrow hands were under mine, and she had the goat. I scuttled to my feet and we both just made it off the road as the car whizzed past, honking long and loud.

"Oh god. It smells!" Vanessa stood with her arms out, and the goat dangled sadly.

The boy disappeared again into more heaving and retching.

"Take it. Take it!" Vanessa screamed.

But I was paralyzed. My arms and the front of my dress were all dark with blood, drying already like smelly paint, and I couldn't move. Balled up in one hand was the shredded remains of my underskirt.

"Just—put it down!" I said.

But Vanessa trembled as the goat made a fresh rattling gasp for life.

"I can't, it's all mangled!"

"Put it on the grass!"

"It's running down my arm!"

"Just here, put it down!"

"MAKE IT STOP!"

Her eyes rolled. She was on the verge of completely losing it. I had to do something, something to make it all stop, to stop that horrible noise at least. I didn't think, I just had to stop the noise. Now. And before I knew what I was doing, I balled up the material in my hand and pressed it to the creature's sodden nose and mouth. Held it. For long enough to see it all happen, as if in slow motion, from a distance, and to think, no this can't be happening. The creature squeaked—and wriggled in Vanessa's arms as she let out a siren scream, and then just as suddenly as it started, she stopped, and everyone seemed to go limp.

Silence.

I stepped back. What have I done now? I couldn't look Vanessa in the face.

"Is it dead?"

"I think so."

Together, we guided the goat down onto the soft grass. Together, we laid her down and carefully brought the neck and limbs into a position that was . . . right, and recognizable, at least. The worst mangling still seemed to be beneath. Neither of us dared to look, but we laid her out as gently as we could, then stood together. I reached out my bloody hand for Vanessa's, and we stood there together on the edge of the light, still panting, still smelling the animal meaty smell of the thing, but somehow that didn't seem so dreadful anymore. It was just sad. We stood there as a whiff of breeze cooled our hot faces, and our shaken breath, and Vanessa's gulping sobs.

The boy loomed up out of the darkness into our circle.

"Oh my god. Choc-Top."

"Choc-Top?" Stupidly shocked that this goat had a name. As it slowly dawned on me that this wasn't a surreal, random nightmare, but a real situation, that these two were already up to their necks in before I even showed up.

**Vanessa Nguyen's letter to the manager of the Pacific Crest Hotel**

*Dear Mr. Chakrabarti,*

*My name is Vanessa Nguyen and I am the mastermind, chief architect, and operative behind the disruption at your hotel last Friday night. I would like to extend my sincerest apology to you and the rest of your staff for the damage and mayhem. It is I who is at fault, and I alone. My cousin Elroy Tran, who until recently was in your employ as a kitchen hand, was but an innocent pawn in my plans. I respectfully ask that you reinstate him as soon as possible. He has done nothing wrong. At all times in his (tangential) involvement in this business, he has behaved respectfully and soberly in the very best interests of you, his employer. I offer this account of the evening not as an excuse or justification for my own terrible behavior but as an exoneration of Elroy. I beg your patience and forbearance as I plead on Elroy's behalf.*

*Many months ago, I forged a plan to deliberately disrupt the proceedings of the school ball. Please forgive me my antipathy toward this ritual. It is my own ideological stance; a reaction against a lifetime of consuming sexist, outdated, culturally irrelevant, consumer-driven capitalist propaganda. As a child of working-class immigrants, I have felt both mocked and isolated by the hysteria surrounding this pantomime, in which I was expected to participate, yet destined forever to be an outsider. I felt compelled to resist, both as an action to raise awareness of my plight and of those like me, and to invite discussion, to challenge the underlying cultural assumptions behind its dominating ethos. I recognize now that the way I chose to address this was wrong; however, to my young mind at the time, I was acting in good faith. In the ardor of my convictions, I was unable to clearly foresee the consequences of my actions. I wanted engagement and recognition, and mistakenly sought these in an act of aggression against my unwitting classmates, which sadly backfired on the most innocent of bystanders, Choc-Top the Goat.*

*Yet I never intended to attack. Inspired by the nonviolent philosophy of leaders such as Martin Luther King Jr. and the transgressive style of performance artist Marina Abramović, I conceived a hybrid art installation/protest in which I would stand silently at the entrance to the ball with a small flock of sheep. My intention was to inspire thought, not fear or even action. I wanted to challenge proceedings by reflecting an uncomfortable reality back to participants, in silence and peace. This would then inspire an internal response; a thought process unique to each individual. My plan was never to interrupt or interfere with the event in any way, except through symbolic imagery. The best I would hope for would be the smallest of intellectual shifts: a little enlightenment, a tiny nudge. This was the extent of my ambition.*

*On the fateful day, I asked my cousin Elroy if he could give me a lift to the hotel. Our families were dining together that evening as is their Friday custom. I was going to the city alone, ostensibly to meet with friends. He was driving in to work. His employment at the venue of our school ball was irrelevant, and entirely coincidental. He was unaware of my plans, or even that my school ball was being held at his workplace. Upon arrival at the hotel, he parked the car, and I agreed to meet him back there when he finished work at midnight. He did not ask where I was going; I did not tell. If he had known my plans beforehand, I doubt he would have supported me to the extent he did—nor offered to drive me into town in the first place. He is a year older than I, and while we are friendly within the family, he is not my confidant.*

*My only confidant in this plan was my friend Dev Khoury, whose name I mention as both my defense witness and my chief accuser. He knew of the plan and weeks before had agreed to source the sheep for the intervention, and participate in it with me. On the night in question, we arranged to meet in the park adjacent to the hotel and it is thither I directed my steps after leaving Elroy at the hotel. It is at this point that my original plan began to unravel, due to circumstances at least partly beyond my control. Dev was very late. By the time he arrived, it was too late for us to stand sentinel at the hotel doors. Even more crucially, he had been unable to secure the sheep as promised, and instead came to the park with a single goat. As a conceptual artist, I was very concerned that the message would be significantly compromised, if not completely derailed, by the substitution. I am not familiar with domestic animals generally; I am interested in their symbolic rather than literal value. I was initially very concerned that the "flocking" behavior commonly attributed to sheep was not shared by goats, also that goats have very different metaphoric and literal connotations, the latter being mostly concerned with the occult. This is not at all the message I wished to convey.*

*If circumstances had not overtaken us at this point, it is highly likely that I would have put a stop to the entire endeavor on those grounds alone. However, the goat escaped from us in the park by slipping its collar. Despite our best efforts to retrieve it, the goat wandered onto the road and was fatally struck by a speeding car. There was nothing any of us could have done. Rest assured that whatever other consequences I may endure from this night of folly, the most enduring punishment of all will be the memory of the poor creature's suffering and death, which I will carry with me for the rest of my life.*

## AMY'S JOURNAL

"She's supposed to be home by ten," the boy said accusingly to Vanessa.

"We were never going to get her home by ten," Vanessa spat back.

"You know this goat?" I asked.

"What am I supposed to say now?" the boy continued, still ignoring me.

"What are you looking at me for?"

"Why would you bring a goat?" I continued.

"I never asked for a goat," Vanessa protested.

"Oh my god," I gasped. "Was this a sacrifice?"

The witchy outfit, the eyeliner, the '70s suit, the aesthetic—it all fit.

Vanessa just looked angrily at the boy. "See, I told you."

"You did this on purpose," I continued.

"You killed it," Vanessa shot back at me with venom.

"I was trying to help."

"There's limits to what you can achieve in taffeta."

"It's silk chiffon."

"I don't give a shit! What are you even doing here?"

"Vanessa—" the boy interjected.

"Shut up, Dev," she flung back. My god, what an absolute bitch!

"Please, let's just—" I started.

"Let's just not," she interrupted me.

"I think we all have been through a traumatic experience; we need to decompress."

"You think? You THINK? No you don't. You wear, you pose, you post. How many likes you got so far tonight?"

Wow. The photo and the ballroom of laughing spectators, momentarily obliterated from my mind by the car crash, came back and fell on my raw heart with a fresh weight.

"Go back to the ball, Killer Kardashian," Vanessa snarled.

I stood rooted to the spot and stared at her, outraged that she could be so cruel.

What do you say to that? What do you say to a witchy bitch who deliberately brought a sacrificial goat to a Year 12 formal, then made you kill it?

The goat lay at our feet. She looked peaceful now, her eyes closed, and she lay as though sleeping on the grass. I briefly knelt down and stroked her face.

"I'm sorry, Choc-Top."

I turned my back on Vanessa and her ghoulish minion, crossed back over the road, picked up my shoes, and walked slowly into the darkness of the opposite field. Tears stung my eyes.

"You should be sorry!" Vanessa shouted after me.

"Shut up," said the boy.

"Murderer!"

"Shut the fuck up, Vanessa!" I heard him say.

I slowed my steps in the dark and resisted the urge to turn around—I wouldn't give her the satisfaction—but I had to listen. Luckily the breeze was going my way.

"Don't talk to me like that!" she blazed.

"You'd rather I call you a dumb fuck?"

"I never call you a dumb fuck!"

"You do it all the time!"

"Well when you act like one—"

"I get you tickets to the ball, a car, livestock, and what do you do? Attack the Good Samaritan."

"She's a mean girl!"

"That's literally the point; Samaritans were historically reviled, which is why—"

"Your niche religious knowledge is irrelevant here, Dev! I just witnessed a fatal car accident."

"So did I."

"My creative vision has been completely ruined."

"Your creative vision sucks."

"That's not what you said yesterday."

"It's dumb *and* impractical."

"'Ooh, Vanessa, I love it! Let's do it, let's protest! It'll be awesome! I can get a sheep, I can get heaps of sheep! You want sheep, I got sheep. Just tell me where and when and how many!'"

"I told you, I only couldn't get the sheep 'cause they were down the paddock!"

"This is not a sheep!"

"It's more than you got!"

"And now it's dead, and you're acting like it's all my fault!"

"It is your fault! You asked for it, you deal with it."

"I did not ask for this!"

"Address and phone number are on the tag."

"Hey! You can't just—"

"Byeeee!"

I could hear him cross the road toward me. I sped up a little so he wouldn't know I was loitering and listening.

"Where are you even going?" she shouted after him.

"To a banal ritual for Americanized sheep-flocking consumer stupid idiots. Because that's what I am. And you wish you were." His footsteps were on the grass behind me now. "Good luck with your conceptual protest!" I slowed down to let him pass and he overtook me without even breaking his stride. "Is that a Victor Drummoyne?" I nodded blankly. "It's nice." He kept going and soon disappeared into the darkness and the distant strains of laughter and music, just a silhouette against the lights from the hotel. Dev. His name is Dev. He's weird, and he was no help with the goat, but he stood up to his friend when she was going off, and that makes him a hero.

"Fine, go then!" screeched Vanessa after him. "My cousin's got a car anyway! And I still have my political integrity! You loser! You dumb fuck!"

There was enough distance between us now for me to turn and actually feel a bit sorry for her. Abandoned by her only friend, just as I had been. Ritual for Americanized sheep. I got it now—they wanted to take sheep to the ball and ruin it, deliberately. To make us all feel as though we were only there because everyone else was there, that we hadn't thought for ourselves, and that the whole thing was culturally irrelevant, driven by conspicuous consumption, and essentially meaningless.

Like I wasn't feeling that already.

She bent over the goat, as though trying to size up how to move it or whether to move it at all. The sight was too sad. I could still feel the sensation of carrying the broken body and the moisture on my hand from pressing against its protesting mouth. I turned to follow Dev back up the hill, but my feet hit something hard and plastic on the grass, and I nearly fell over some random contraption of wheels and metal and fabric. What the hell? I sprang back instinctively—too many surprises tonight already—then I saw that it was an old stroller. A real one, not a toy one, that had been abandoned on the playing fields.

"Dev!" Vanessa screeched on the wind. "I can't move it by myself!"

I reached down and righted the stroller. Gave it a little push. One wonky wheel. But it still worked. The words "Killer Kardashian" echoed in my ears.

I didn't go back for Vanessa. I went back for Choc-Top.

8

**Vanessa Nguyen's letter to the manager of the Pacific Crest Hotel**

*Dev was shattered by the experience of witnessing the accident and the goat's subsequent demise. As I believe is not uncommon under such circumstances, Dev disengaged from the situation and, rightly or wrongly, abandoned me to deal with it as best I could. He chose to retreat to the familiar by going to the ball. I do not judge him for this, as mental health is of utmost importance, especially for young people, and he needed to take time to process events. However, he did leave me alone with the goat and no means of transportation. I realize with the benefit of hindsight that I should at this point have appealed for adult assistance. However, at the time, I felt responsible for the situation and unwilling to involve anyone else. I believed the most expeditious and humane course of action was to remove the goat from the scene and dispose of it myself, using my cousin's vehicle for transport. No doubt I was not thinking rationally, possibly due to shock and the trauma of the event, otherwise it would have occurred to me to arrange to bring the car to the animal, rather than the animal to the car.*

## AMY'S JOURNAL

I stood there with my stroller, too scared to say anything. She just looked at me with contempt, and for a split second I thought she was going to swear at me again. But she turned away in disgust instead, so I ignored her right back, knelt down by the goat, and tried to drag the sack of its body up into the stroller.

"Put it on its side," Vanessa muttered.

I took this as an apology. I put the stroller down on its side, and together we rolled the goat in like some kind of very lumpy, meaty doll and levered the stroller back upright again.

"Where to now?" I asked.

"My cousin's car."

Vanessa pointed up the hill at the hotel looming over the playing fields.

I leaned in to push the stroller, but with the extra weight, the bad wheel, and the rough grass, it was a bumpy ride.

"Grass is bad."

"Footpath," ordered Vanessa.

So in silence, side by side, we heaved the stroller over to the footpath beside the road and then started the long, rattly ride along the footpath, the long way back to the hotel, via the street. Just us, the streetlights, the distant whoosh of the main roads, and our stroller with the goat. The two weirdest parents you ever did see. And with this new identity came a new perspective, from which the breadth of my years at school—that had always seemed too vast and varied and dramatic to even contemplate as a whole—dwindled down to something quite neat. The ongoing roller coaster of my entire life suddenly looked extremely conventional and sheltered and quiet, as though I had never really been alive before. All the hopes I'd had for tonight to be beautiful and perfect, and for myself to be the queen of the evening, had all crashed and dissolved into nothing. And with all of it gone, I felt free. This was the real me, the inevitable core. Limping along a footpath on the side of a road at the edge of an unwelcoming city, barefoot, with stinging knees, driving myself through squares of light and oblongs of darkness, with a girl I'd been at school with for years and years and never really spoken to.

"Did you go to my primary school?"

"Yes. Years Four, Five, and Six."

"Were you in my class?"

"Years Four and Five I was."

"Really?"

"No, I'm lying. Yes really."

"Where did you sit?"

"The back."

"Oh."

More silence, more rattling.

"So they moved you to the . . . other class in Year Six?"

She knew what I meant. There was the good class and the other class.

"I asked to be moved."

Clearly a lie.

"Why would you do that? That was the top class, Miss Secombe was amazing, Year Six was—just—great. With her. There was a whole gang of girls—"

"I didn't like that gang."

I was about to defend them, but then from here, in the dark, I could see them, all curled up into a snippy, self-satisfied little pack. Vanessa was right. They weren't that great anymore. They seemed petty and small. The kind of girls who would put hours—days—weeks of preparation into an outfit, and no thought at all into a hurtful slight.

"But . . . it was the top class. You're smart, Vanessa. I know you're smart."

"It was the top class out of two. Doesn't count for much. Anyway. Do you know who came top in the school?"

I knew it wasn't me, or any of my friends, and I knew we had been a bit surprised, and privately I was more than a bit annoyed. But I couldn't remember who it was.

"You did," I realized.

"I did."

And yet now, I didn't even mind. It all seemed so very pointless.

"I'm going to do law," Vanessa announced quietly to the darkness. "At one of the top unis in Australia. I haven't decided which one."

"I was thinking of law too."

"But I'm going to get the grades to do medicine."

Wow. Arrogant. No friends. My benevolent feelings toward her shriveled, despite our shared predicament and my own friendlessness. There's no point being nice to someone who doesn't appreciate it. But then again, what is nice? I thought my friends were nice, I thought tonight would be nice. I was beginning to doubt whether I could identify the quality of niceness anymore, or whether I ever could. Here in the dark, everything was shifting, nothing sat properly. My insides were as messed up as the goat.

On we trudged, up the hill, out of the park, past a couple of old low-rise office buildings, toward a more brightly lit street, where we would turn and walk to the hotel. Past more office blocks, closed cafés, maybe even a bar or two. And me looking like this, and the goat—surely we're not doing this?

"Is there another way we can go?"

"I don't think so."

"There's a car!" I shrank away into the shadows.

"They can't even see us!"

But it seemed to be slowing! We scurried behind a handy tree as a white car slid to a stop at the curb close behind us. We lurked in the shadows like criminals and listened as two car doors opened and slammed, and a familiar voice called out a very familiar name.

"Leo!"

I jumped. It was a voice from the school corridor, from the classroom. From Miss Starkey. My eyebrows shot up, my eyes pressed wide in the darkness as they met a similar surprised gleam from Vanessa. I must have squeaked in shock. Vanessa pressed a finger to her lips. Footsteps, running, as the body of the voice of Miss Starkey must have chased after person she had called Leo. But not very far. He stopped, the running stopped, just on the other side of our handy shrub, close enough for us to hear the slide of hands on clothes.

"Text me when you get to the after-party and I'll come pick you up."

## Elizabeth Starkey's Statement to Police

My car keys and parking ticket were in my clutch purse that whole time. I couldn't tell you what happened to them or my car for that hour or so. As far as I knew, my car was safe in the parking lot. At the end of the night my keys were in my purse and there was a ticket that I assumed was the one from the start of the night, but I never looked at it closely so it very easily could have been replaced. I'm not pointing fingers but basically anyone could have stolen my keys and the ticket, and taken my car out, pretending to be me. I was wearing a long black outfit and my hair was down, and there were at least 15 girls there that night who answered that description at our event alone. It could have been any one of them. It certainly wasn't me.

## AMY'S JOURNAL

My mouth fell open.

"I'm going with my friends, so . . ." mumbled Leo. Leo. My Leo. Mumbling up close to Miss Starkey.

"So ditch them. Come to my place." She's actually inviting him to her place. Like it's no big deal. I smacked my hands over my mouth to stop from shouting out "OH MY FREAKING GOD."

"You need to work with me on this relationship, babe," she continued.

Vanessa was so freaked out that she seemed almost about to laugh. It was the most animated I'd ever seen her.

"Fine," muttered Leo.

"We have this connection, you know, and it's deep. We've got to honor that."

More sounds of hands on clothes, of hands on a face, of leaning in, of kissing?

"I'll see you later then?" she said. With a touch of aggression, like she was annoyed she wasn't getting her own way. Being rejected by Leo? Oh my god, I felt her pain.

"I don't want to see you later," he said.

Shit, Leo. What have you gotten yourself into?

"Yes you do."

There's the teacher voice again.

"I don't want to see you at all," he said with more conviction than I'd heard from him in a year.

"Seriously? Why? Because you made me hit a goat?"

Now Vanessa's mouth fell open in outrage too, and something that had already dropped fell even further in the pit of my stomach.

"No."

"That is so immature."

Footsteps. He's leaving, he's heading back to the hotel.

"All right then, piss off back to your stupid party."

And he did. He kept walking. But she shouted after him.

"Hey, you can't just do that, you know. You can't just walk away."

But his footsteps were getting farther away. He was walking away, he was doing it.

"We're adults, Leo, we need to communicate!"

He stopped, a few meters away now.

"I'm not going to chase you!" But he kept walking. Miss Starkey turned back to the car. "Fucking asshole," she spat under her breath as she retreated. The car door slammed, the engine gunned—with the same evil cough that left Choc-Top for dead—and she roared off.

Gone, down Lark Street, back toward the hotel.

"Oh my fucking GOD," exploded Vanessa.

And Leo's footsteps stopped. He turned as the car whooshed off, walked toward our bush, and swung his steps away from the curb so he could peer around it. And there we were. All of us. He was right there, in his suit, and we stared at each other in utter shock. We stepped out from the shadows. The busted stroller wheel scraped pathetically along concrete. And we all just continued to stare.

"It was your goat," he said finally.

"It was her car," said Vanessa.

"It was her," said I.

I was surprised that my voice sounded solid and mature, not at all on the edge of tears. I wasn't devastated. I was almost relieved. In my mind, this mythical other girl was sophisticated and beautiful and funny and everything I thought I was, but had then been so thoroughly proven not to be. But that wasn't the case at all. It was someone all too real, not particularly good-looking, and hopelessly mundane. A teacher. A *teacher*. We all knew it, and it was sickening. Despite the pornographic photo, the dead goat, and the blood-stained dress, Leo was in more trouble than I was that night. We sat in the horror of it all, and still Leo tried to backpedal, with all the energy of a liar. And suddenly I realized how very comprehensively Leo had lied not only to me, but to the whole school, which is, as far as we're concerned, the entire world.

"Look, I don't know what you think you heard—" he started, but he stopped just as suddenly as he began when another car slid into the space where Miss Starkey's car had just been with a sudden burst of a siren. We were all bathed in a splash of red and blue light. The cops. I felt Leo and Vanessa straighten into defense mode, just as if a teacher had walked into a classroom full of unsupervised kids going nuts. I didn't even have time to think how weird this was, that Leo, always a rebel, had secretly been on the teachers' side. Literally. Anyway, I had never been a rebel, secretly or otherwise, and the siren filled me with nothing but relief. Finally. I love the moment when the teacher walks in. I have always been a great believer in the power of rules. They give structure, they make everything run smoother, they point the way to your goals, they distinguish the rule-breakers and give everyone a very clear mechanism for getting rid of them. And so many rules had been broken, I just felt exhausted. I wanted someone to take charge, take this all out of our hands and sort it out. It was time to call in the adults, and if that meant throwing my new partners in crime under the bus, then so be it.

9

## Constable McAvoy's Report

At approximately 7:19 p.m. on the night of April 14, I was proceeding on a routine patrol through the city area when on the corner of Hill and Lark Streets I was alerted to the presence of three young people loitering on the footpath area.

I slowed the vehicle to observe more closely and observed that they were a male and two female persons in what appeared to be fancy dress with a puppet or toy stuffed animal in a stroller or pram, or possibly a kind of go-cart. I took this in good faith as it is not unusual to see young people in fancy dress, in a Halloween-related costume or similar, particularly during the warmer months. I recall it was warm on that evening. As I pulled up alongside the persons, I did not observe any suspicious behavior. They did not appear to be drinking or under the influence of alcohol or drugs of any kind, however it is my job as a police officer to monitor behavior of young people in public, particularly after hours, and I am required by law to do so.

## AMY'S JOURNAL

The driver's-side window whirred downward and out popped the face of a guy who looked just like a kindly sergeant on an Australian TV dramedy, with laughter lines, graying temples, a benevolent smile, and a bit of a gruff edge. The kind of guy who has a vulnerable side but you just know he's going to lose it at someone later in the episode, and everyone will get scared. Thinks he's everyone's tough-but-fair dad.

Vanessa suddenly jerked the stroller from my hand and stepped in front of it, blocking the officer's view of Choc-Top.

"All right?" said the officer. The others replied both at once, in a pitch an octave higher than usual.

"Yes, thank you," smiled Vanessa.

"Yep, all good," offered Leo.

"Are you kidding me?" I exploded. I couldn't even be bothered taking in their outraged looks and silent, desperate direction to shut the fuck up. Like, no. This is an emergency.

"I'm so glad you're here because to be honest this is all getting way out of control," I told the officer. I even had my hand on the car. "This *boy* is in a relationship with his Math teacher."

"Whoa! I have NO idea what—" protested Leo, while Vanessa tried to pull me back and was saying something about me being a little bit overexcited.

"Get off! *She* is planning some kind of terrorist attack."

"That is ridiculous!" interrupted Vanessa.

I squirmed away from her and closer to the car.

"And I am a murderer. No kidding. I did it." I pointed at the goat. "See? That was me. You have to take us all to the station."

"I see," nodded the officer, with one of those very raspy, gravelly voices from years of telling people off. "That's all pretty serious stuff."

"And my best friend Gabby Gibson has been distributing naked photos. Child porn." Might as well get it all dealt with at once. And that shut Vanessa up pretty fast.

"Looks like you should all be under arrest then," said the officer with a contemplative nod. "Hey?"

We all stared at him, me with determined acceptance, the others with horror. In my mind we were already in some terrible fluorescent-lit, laminate-tiled processing room at the station, getting a pat-down and putting our precious things in ziplock plastic bags. And waiting while they called our parents. Oh god. It was one thing to rat out to the police. Parents were worse. Leo and Vanessa were never ever going to forgive me for this, but I would have to stand strong. After all, whatever I was guilty of (I was still not quite sure what that was—"murder" seemed a little much), I knew I was on the way to owning it and fixing it. Leo and Vanessa needed to step up.

The officer contemplated the three of us—and the stroller—with the look of a man who is quite comfortable making people wait for him to speak. "Too bad there's no law against excessive drama." And he burst into a scratchy heave of silent laughter, along with the younger officer in the passenger's seat, who until then had been looking at something else. I think it might have been his phone. "Seriously though," he added, and the laughter dropped away as fast as it had appeared. "Get back to the school social before I pick you up for loitering."

I stared at him in disbelief.

"It's what he would have wanted," he said, pointing at Choc-Top. Then he winked, the window whirred back up, he tooted the horn in a friendly thanks-for-having-us-over-for-lunch kind of way, and the police car was gone. And it was just the three of us again, still standing on the side of the road with a stroller full of mangled goat.

## Constable McAvoy's Report

I addressed the young people, I believe something along the lines of "Good evening" or "Are you having a good night?" One of the young females answered in the affirmative then proceeded to make a series of claims which were of a frivolous and preposterous nature. This is not unheard of when police officers approach young people and I am experienced in "reading the room" so to speak in such situations. I answered in a jocular manner appropriate to the jocularity of the young female, something along the lines of "That's very funny" or "I believe you are joking." I then encouraged all three persons to return to their social engagement, which I correctly deduced to be a school ball held at the Pacific Crest Hotel approximately 100 meters further down Lark Street traveling in a northerly direction.

At no time did I have any reason to suspect a crime of any kind had been committed or that the young people were in danger or had been in any danger at any point.

It was a little bit dark owing to it being night at the time, which could have contributed to my assessment of the situation.

## AMY'S JOURNAL

Luckily all three of us felt the best way to deal with what had just happened was to ignore it completely.

"That wheel's fucked," announced Vanessa to Leo. "Help us carry it?"

"Yeah," he mumbled. And so the three of us hoisted the

stroller like it was a sacred offering in the worst ever ceremonial procession, and walked in and out of the blobs of street light all the way back up the deserted city sidewalk to the hotel. We were no longer worried about being caught—we'd already been caught fair and square—but it seemed our crimes were so fantastical that we were beyond the reach of the law. If nobody believed it, did it even happen? Would there be any consequences, beyond scabby knees and a ruined Victor Drummoyne? For everyone else, the night at the ballroom was most likely proceeding just as planned, in a kind of parallel world of perfection. Perhaps there was a chance we would get out of this mess unscathed after all.

**Chat: Gabby, Amy**
**Friday, April 14, 7:35 p.m.**

**Gabby:** Amy me Bianca and Kate r worried about u

**Gabby:** R u ok? The park is dangerous Kate said one time someone was murdered there

**Gabby:** Pls don't be mad at me

**Gabby:** Everyone's asking me where u r

**Gabby:** Pls reply to me Amy I'm really worried about u ur my best friend ever

**Gabby:** Pls be safe and come back intime for the presentation bc Ms Kruger was asking

**Gabby:** <3

##  Gabby Gibson's Email to the Principal—Page 4

I tried to get Amy to come back to the ball and I sent her like a million texts but she didn't reply, for all I know she was out in the dark getting raped and murdered. But I felt really terrible and when I sat there looking around at everyone else having fun and everything, and laughing about Amy, I got quite mad. I just wanted them to know that Amy is actually a great girl and a really good friend. She wouldn't laugh at anyone like that. She wouldn't. She's always very kind and helpful and caring and she really cares a lot about things like the environment and school spirit. While I was sitting there watching everyone else I wanted them to know that. I wanted to somehow tell them that Amy is a very good friend and didn't deserve being treated like just a joke or a meme. I started flicking through all the pics on my phone of us having fun together. I have a whole album of like hundreds of pics that are all us having fun. It made me cry almost to look at them all because they start right back in Year 7 when she had short hair. That was when I had the idea of changing the photos on the slideshow display.

## Chris Butt's Incident Report

The night was pretty normal, the kids behaved good, there's always a few ratbags isn't there who popped balloons and so forth but I say good luck to them, it's their night, they pay for any damage anyway and those balloons didn't even belong to the hotel and it's not like they're meant to be permanent so what's the harm. But that girl in green, she was a bit of a sneaky one if you know what I mean because she came back up later and started chatting to me about this and that and asking questions about school balls and things. I make a point of not socializing with the hirers because that's not my job and it's policy. I definitely did not encourage her in any way but she was just chatting, which I realized later was a deliberate ploy because that must be when she changed the input over to her phone and I was taking care of a million other things as usual, which is why she was able to do it, or she might have had help from one of the boys probably but I don't know. I didn't see anyone else get near the desk and in seven years of doing this job I've never had anyone tamper with the equipment and we've done some balls and had some functions for pretty rough people including a biker gang and they never did anything like that. I'm shocked to be honest with you.

## Gabby Gibson's Email to the Principal—Page 5

I didn't think Amy would even do the presentation. I thought she might never come back. So I thought I would do it. If she wasn't there I would have to get up and talk to the whole school, and I would talk about what a good friend Amy is, and then I would show all the photos on my phone of us, and it would be beautiful, and it would make them stop laughing at her and maybe think. A bit. I don't know, I wasn't thinking too hard about it at the time but it seemed like a good idea and normally I talk things over with Amy and there was no way I was telling Kate and Bianca. As far as I was concerned they were canceled.

I went up to the tech guy and started chatting with him about school balls and stuff. I was just trying to distract him a bit really, like I was a spy or something. But we ended up having kind of an interesting conversation. He said school balls were all boring, he's been to so many of them at the hotel, and they all look the same. And I said yes but everybody only normally gets one, and it's their special night, and he said he didn't even go to his own ball. Which made me wonder. I mean, we were all so looking forward to it and it seemed like such a big deal and here was someone who didn't even bother going. I don't know anyone in our cohort who didn't go. In fact I even thought you had to go if you were enrolled, like doing an exam or something, but turns out you don't at all. It's just something fun. Which made me wonder if I would have wanted to go if I ever really thought we had a choice. And in the end this is kind of interesting because as it turned out the whole night was a total disaster and not what anyone wanted at all, so really we're just like the tech guy because we might as well not have had one, everything went so wrong.

Anyway while we were talking I stood with my back to the tech desk and I slipped the flash drive out and plugged my phone in and he totally didn't even see me do that. It was probably the best moment of the whole night for me. I made sure my phone was set so that it would run on my little album of pics of me and Amy and then I went back to my table, which was even more boring and sad than before because now I didn't even have my phone to play with, and I couldn't finish my dinner. I'm sorry Ms. Kruger, but I think you should know that the veggie lasagna was the worst.

SCHOOL COMMUNITY NEWSLETTER

## FROM THE PRINCIPAL'S DESK

The night proceeded as per planned until the start of the presentation and I personally, along with everyone else in the ballroom, was unaware of anything out of the ordinary until then. I had been assured earlier in the night that the presentation, as planned and approved by me and the Committee, would proceed as normal. It featured a series of very nice photos of our school grounds and the cohort's achievements over the last six years, including sports carnivals, our excellent productions of *Hairspray* and *Fiddler on the Roof*, the award-winning performance at the Jazz Festival, and a tribute to our Debate Team and Math Club. Amy Middleton had prepared a speech that was to congratulate the students on successful completion of their junior year of schooling, welcome everyone to the challenges and joys of our final year together, and wish them well in the spirit of collegial respect. It is a source of great disappointment to me that this speech was never delivered, as I believe it directly addresses many of the issues which, had you all paid attention as you should, would have prevented the situations and circumstances that led to this very upsetting result.

## ✉ Gabby Gibson's Email to the Principal—Page 6

When you came up to me and asked me where Amy was and I said she was in the bathroom, I'm really sorry I was actually lying. But things were already getting a bit crazy and people over at the tables near the windows had popped all of their balloons so I know you were pretty mad about that and the other people who were touching things they shouldn't have and some people were kissing a lot, which I know isn't appropriate behavior at a formal event. I didn't want to worry you even more than you were clearly actually very worried already. So I didn't say anything and I know now that I should have said something maybe but then who knows. It probably wouldn't have made any difference anyway but I am sorry, so there's that. I didn't know for sure that Amy wouldn't show up as I had no idea where she was, so in a way it also would have been lying to say that she had gone. My plan was just going to be that when you made the announcement, then I would get up.

I was as surprised as everyone else when she walked in.

I was not expecting it at all.

10

## AMY'S JOURNAL

Vanessa led us up a concrete driveway that curled around the back of the hotel to a service entrance that smelled of garbage and laundry detergent. Her face was buried in her phone, her thumb moved like lightning as she texted, but that didn't stop her from finding fault and barking out instructions. "This way." "Carry it properly." "Slow the fuck down." She is very bossy, which I know is not a feminist word but it definitely applies best to the way she was bossing us around. The driveway ended with a ramp to a huge platform, like a stage, littered with carts of laundry bags and delivery pallets and industrial stuff. At the back of the platform were large rubbery swinging double doors—the staff entrance to the hotel.

"Down now," Vanessa instructed. "My cousin'll be here in a minute." She flung us a combative stare, and Leo and I stared right back.

In the yellow industrial light, we all looked a bit sick and bleary. I don't know about Leo, but I would have preferred just to stay on a never-ending journey of goat-carrying. The light was shining on more than just the dumpster bins—it was putting a spotlight back on all the crappy situations we'd fled.

"You can just go back now. I'm fine; I don't need you anymore," she said, like a teacher dismissing us. We didn't move. "Thanks, by the way."

Vanessa looked up from her phone as she said this, and as she looked at me, her habitual expression of general distaste turned into an actual face of eww-that's-gross. Leo followed her gaze to me and did the same. Revulsion. At me. They were looking at ME like I was something disgusting that had been dragged out of a sewer.

"Oh god," said Vanessa.

"What?" I looked down at my hands, and my dress. Oh god is right. The sequin embellishment, the delicate embroidery, the sheen of rose-quartz crystal chiffon was all but obliterated by smears and gobs of dark crimson and brown blood. My hands actually looked like I was wearing gloves from the back, although somehow along the way I must have wiped the palms as they were now a shade of clay and my skirt was looped with stripes of gore and crunchy bunches of it where I must have balled the skirt up to hitch it or rip it or god knows what.

"Oh," I said, like a complete idiot. And tears sprang to my eyes again, and I couldn't touch my face with my hands, because suddenly they felt all hot and dry and disgusting, so the tears just welled up and caught bits of hair and rolled down my cheeks.

"Wow," said Leo, totally unhelpfully. "The full Stephen King." And then I started to gulp and sob. "Sorry."

Vanessa sighed deeply. I could see her clearly too, now that we were in full light, and she was pretty much in the same predicament as me but somehow in a black tunic, black lace, and combat boots, the smears of blood were hardly noticeable, and if anything they looked like mud and gave her rather an air of capable authority. She whipped off the black sweater she had tied around her waist and held it out to me.

"Here." I was whimpering too much to take it. "Arms up," she instructed, and I obeyed because I had clearly reverted to the emotional age of a toddler. She pulled the sweater over my head and down over my front. "There," she said. It was thin, probably cheap, but it was one of those long draped knits with a few choice holes and tears in it that made it fall in a way that was actually quite attractive. I was still gulping and sobbing, but I could use the sleeve to wipe away some of the snot at least.

"It's almost like it was meant to be like that," added Leo, as if I cared about his fucking approval anymore. I was back swimming in all the horrors of the night—less than two hours ago I was on top of the world, thinking I was just one kiss away from perfection, and now here I was with gloves of blood and a cheap black sweater, standing next to a dumpster, and those things weren't even the worst of it. I burst into a fresh, inconsolable hiccup of full-on ugly crying like I don't think I've done since I was ten.

"Come on, it's only a dress!" said Vanessa.

I turned on her with dripping red-faced fury. "I don't care about the stupid dress, okay?" I yelled. "And you're totally paying for the cleaning."

Like cleaning was even possible.

Leo rubbed my shoulder in a comforting way. "Look, we can go back in, find a bathroom somewhere, fix you up," he said. I shoved him away. "We'll forget all about it." He held his hand out to me. "Come on, I'll make it up to you. I promise."

"I can't go back in there!" I snapped.

"Sure you can. Nobody knows about any of this. A bit of a wash—"

"You haven't seen your phone, have you?"

"What?"

"Just check it."

He took his phone out of his pocket. Must have had it on silent in the car with Miss Starkey. Typical. Teachers hate phones. Of course it took him about two and a half seconds to land on the photo of me with my undies around my ankles. Less. And his face did exactly what you'd expect a teenage boy's face to do at the sight of it. It was sickening—disbelief turning to dirty, smirky delight that he wanted to hide but couldn't. I have never hated him so much as I did in that moment. But more than that, I hated myself, for how reduced I was. Nothing more than a filthy photo and a joke.

Leo tried to cover up. "Oh. Ohh. That's—that's nasty, that is."

"You should have hit me with that car."

"What? What is it?" Vanessa snatched the phone out of Leo's hand and took a good look. I just couldn't face it and collapsed into a squat on the concrete floor with my arms wrapped around my head.

"I'll get her an Uber," I heard Leo say.

"Why?" shot back Vanessa, with her usual dry aggression.

I looked up. I expected her to be gloating, but she wasn't. She was holding the phone and looking from Leo to me with detached hostility, mixed with a bit of incomprehension.

"Well, that's her," said Leo, as though that explained why I needed to be removed from the situation, and indeed my life. Which I thought was quite obvious.

"So?"

"So . . . you can see . . . like—"

"Everything," I wailed. "You can see everything." Was Vanessa blind?

"Only if you look."

"Yeah. Everyone's looking," said Leo with finality as he took the phone back and scrolled through the comments.

"That's not her fault." Vanessa reached down and grabbed my arm. "Get up." Again, toddler Amy just wordlessly obeyed. "You haven't done anything wrong. I mean apart from trying to get us arrested, which was pretty low. But this. This is not your fault. And it doesn't matter anyway. It's nothing."

"It's . . . everything," I sputtered.

"It's a picture. It's obviously meant to be private."

"It's embarrassing, it's shameful!"

"No it's not. Sending it is embarrassing. Looking at it is shameful." She turned to Leo, who was still scrolling and trying not to smirk. "Right?" He shoved the phone guiltily back in his pocket.

"Yeah," he said, suddenly serious, reflecting. "Yeah, it is." With the voice of a man. It's so spooky how teenage boys can do that.

And as suddenly as it hit him, it dawned on me too. Could it be that the crappiest thing about all crap on the internet is not the crap itself, but the people who look at it? In a whole night of upside-down revelations, this one actually made a lot of sense. It wasn't me. It was them all along. But before I could fully process this totally bizarre idea, a kind of hot-looking young Asian guy came pelting out of the rubbery doors in a white T-shirt, checked pants, an apron, sweat, and an air of urgency.

*I texted my cousin Elroy and asked him to meet me at the service entrance to the hotel, whither I directed myself and the goat. Matters were further complicated by the presence of some other members of the school cohort who involved themselves in the situation, much against my wishes. On the way to the hotel, one of them even attempted to attract the attention of law enforcement. Due to the well-documented regular mistreatment of people of color by authorities, I concealed the goat from the police, resisted their (minimal) efforts to intimidate us, and retained control of the situation. Indeed, prior to our arrival at the hotel, we had done nothing wrong in any event, apart from allowing the goat to slip its collar, which, as previously explained, was an accident. I did not tell Elroy why I wanted to see him. It was only when he met me that he became aware of my predicament. Naturally, as my cousin, he was very concerned for my welfare and implored me to seek proper help. In my youthful arrogance, I refused, and begged him to allow me to put the goat in his car. This would have solved the most immediate and pressing problem, which was the presence of the corpse. Elroy was reluctant, which I now understand was not just selfishness on his part, but motivated by his desire to seek a more permanent solution.*

"What are you doing here?" he panted. Vanessa just pointed at our stroller of limp goat carcass, and his mouth dropped open. "What the actual—"

"Can we just put it in your car?" she interrupted.

"Seriously?"

"Please?"

"It was kind of my fault," started Leo, but nobody heard.

"Just gimme your keys, Elroy," Vanessa went on, holding out her hand. It seems the bossy approach didn't work so well on a member of her own family.

"You're not putting that in my car."

"What about in there?" She pointed at a big garbage bin.

"Are you kidding? This is a hotel. You can't dump a dead animal!"

She pouted and opened her mouth to launch into a new round of extreme whining but was silenced by Elroy suddenly shushing her. There were two adult voices on the other side of the rubbery door, clearly coming our way.

"Shit!" said Elroy as he leaped into action like we were in some major heist movie. He grabbed a cart full of stacked fresh laundry bags, flung them off, and whipped one of them open. "Put it on there!" he hissed at us as he expertly flicked out a tablecloth. We had just enough time to tip the goat onto the cart and shove the stroller behind the bin as the tablecloth floated down over the corpse. Two kitchen workers emerged, with cigarettes and lighters already in hand.

"Hey dude," said the older one to Elroy.

"Hey," he replied, as though this were the dullest moment of the dullest night at work ever. The workers' eyes scanned us, deadpan, as they flicked on a flame and touched it to their cigarettes. Then they raised their eyebrows at Elroy, drew back, and exhaled together, like this was some kind of performance art and we were all waiting for something to happen. How long does it take to smoke a cigarette? A lot longer than we could all legitimately stand there watching them do it. Especially as now they were looking at the cart.

**Vanessa Nguyen's letter to the manager of the Pacific Crest Hotel**

*While we were discussing the best course of action, two other employees came out of the service entrance. In order to prevent them from discovering the goat, the corpse was placed on a nearby cart of laundry and covered with a tablecloth. This was tacitly understood to be a temporary measure, intended merely to hide it from Elroy's colleagues for a short period of time. Unfortunately, the colleagues proceeded to smoke cigarettes and attempted to engage us in light conversation.*

"It's a special cake," I blurted out, pointing at the cart. It was the only thing I could think of, and I knew it was stupid, but then halfway out of my mouth I realized it was not stupid at all but a pretty good idea. They wouldn't question it if they thought it was something we were in charge of. "Delivery. For the ball."

"Yes," confirmed Elroy, with a palpable sense of relief.

"Cool," said the older worker as he took another judgmental drag on his cigarette. "What kind of cake? Looks huge."

He moved closer. His hand hovered at the corner of the tablecloth, but Elroy grabbed him just in time.

"Dude."

"What?"

"Can you get the cigarette away from the food?"

Apparently it was fine for food to be in this filthy delivery dock, but toxic smoke was a poison too far. And a legitimate concern, because it raised no eyebrows and the older guy just backed away.

"You know where to take it?" he mumbled.

"Yes," Elroy, Vanessa, Leo, and I all chorused together.

"Through to the kitchen," added the guy, in that annoying way adults tell you things even after you've made it clear you don't want or need them to. He opened the rubbery door and gestured inward. We hesitated, trying to think of a legitimate reason to not go, but there was none, and nothing happened for the length of a whole big drag and exhale of the cigarette.

Eventually, Elroy said, "Yeah, come on guys, bring it straight through." He ushered us and the cart through the big rubbery doors, down a concrete corridor that smelled of layers and layers of cooking smells, and straight into an industrial elevator. Nobody could speak to anybody, or look at anybody. We were all living out a spy fantasy scenario and it's nothing at all like you'd expect. We were not cool, cocky, or confident—we were just scared and awkward, very aware that at any second this whole surprise cake scenario could unravel.

"Hold the elevator!" A cozy-looking fortysomething in chef's whites came trotting up with a cart full of individual servings of chocolate mousse. Elroy shoved our goat cart to the back of the elevator and we all lined up in a regiment in front of it, forming a human shield between mousse and goat. We all stared straight ahead and tried not to breathe too much, as though that would make a difference. But the chef didn't seem to notice anything wrong, as she was rather concerned with the little pewter bowls bumping out of their careful arrangement in rows.

"Having a good night, then?" she said sociably.

"Yep," Leo squeaked.

"Best night of my life. School ball. Yes indeedy. Want a mousse?"

Everyone chorused in the negative, except for me, because I totally wanted one. It was written all over my face.

"Go on. You know you want to," she purred at me.

Oh, how I wanted one of those creamy chocolatey pots. I would have grabbed several, but my hands were too crusty. I clasped them behind my back. "I'll have one later," I promised.

"Me too," she said with a wink.

The doors dinged, and the chef cheerily rattled away down the corridor.

"This way," hissed Elroy, and he ushered us down the opposite direction, into the dark, where the sounds of music and social chatter—the sounds of our own school ball—got louder and louder. One more turn and we came to a dead end and a service door.

**Vanessa Nguyen's letter to the manager of the Pacific Crest Hotel**

*Our only avenue of escape was to retreat inside the hotel with the cart and its grisly burden. Of course this was far from ideal and not a course of action that we wanted to take, given the obvious health impacts. Yet Elroy did his absolute best to steer us away from harm and maintain the integrity of the hotel environment by taking us through service corridors that were quite clearly already contaminated, or at the very least not particularly sanitary. He led us to a dark, apparently unused service area where we could wait, unseen and unheard, until he got a proper break. He would then lead us back outside and we would deal with the goat with no threat to the hotel, the staff, the patrons, or ourselves. Elroy acted in good faith, and was very much motivated simply to get back to work. The mayhem that happened next was in no way his fault.*

---

***Transcription of Detective Wozniak's interview with Leo Prince***

**SW:** So you hit the goat and drove off, but then you drove back?

**LEO:** Yeah.

**SW:** And you found the goat on the road?

**LEO:** Well, no. Amy and this other girl from our year, Vanessa, they got it off the road.

**SW:** Amy?

**LEO:** Yeah, it's complicated, but it doesn't matter any-way. I parked the car back in the parking lot—

**SW:** Before you decided to go back for the goat?

**LEO:** Yeah. No. I parked the car, and then I walked back to help Amy and Vanessa with the goat. It was the right thing to do, because . . . because I hit it.

**SW:** How did you find them?

**LEO:** They were hard to miss.

**SW:** And you went back to the hotel after that?

**LEO:** Yeah.

**SW:** With the goat.

**LEO:** Yes, with the goat; it was Vanessa's goat. She was on her way to the ball and then after the accident she met up with Amy and they had to get it back to her cousin's car or something—

**SW:** At the hotel?

**LEO:** Yes, at the hotel. Everything was . . . connected. In a weird way. It's difficult to explain.

**SW:** Try.

## AMY'S JOURNAL

Elroy pulled the cart to a standstill and turned on Vanessa. "I swear if you get me sacked, I'll do to you whatever you did to this goat," he threatened.

"Okay."

"I get a proper break in half an hour. Don't move from here. For god's sake."

"I won't."

Elroy looked us over in the dim, low-ceilinged corridor. Not spies. Just hopeless. He shook his head and left us there, with nothing but the thumping music and swelling roar of chatter from our own classmates, who were all on the other side of that wall. The other side of the door.

It was so dark in the corridor that we could barely see each other. It was just us and the cart, some mighty weird backstage industrial smells, and the bass notes thumping beneath the chatter. We were looming blobs in the shadows, backlit by a green sign of a figure running through an open door. Its glow shot a sliver of light along the handles of the service door that led through to the ballroom. Leo and I folded our arms and leaned against the wall as we settled in for a boring wait ahead. Not Vanessa. She looked around, up, everywhere, as though trying to distract herself from the magnetic pull of the door.

"Don't do it," I hissed at her.

"Do what?" She laid a hand on the service door.

"That!"

"You are such a princess." Like the pink crystal chiffon wasn't already a deep source of pain at that moment, in more ways than one. She pushed the door open with the softest of clunks and pressed her body against the gap so we couldn't see past her. Leo angled himself off the wall and snuck right up behind her to peer over her head. Great. *If you're going to do something that puts all of us at risk, the least you can do is share the benefit.*

The sounds of the pumping ballroom ballooned into our dingy corridor, and I could even pick out individual voices.

Crystal's laugh. Macca yelling across the room. At the closest table, there was a disagreement over who was sitting where. Then the music faded down to nothing, the cacophony of voices swelled a bit, then faded back down as Ms. Kruger boomed out in all her amplified glory, transporting everyone there right back to the assembly hall.

### Elizabeth Starkey's Statement to Police

After my walk I went back to the ballroom. It was close to 8 o'clock, when the speech presentation was about to start. I felt much better by then. I didn't go straight back to my table because Ms. Kruger was speaking, so I stood at the back of the ballroom and watched and supervised the students from there.

## AMY'S JOURNAL

"Settle down, people, thank you. Settle," intoned Ms. Kruger. Of course nobody was ready to settle and the argument over seats seemed to be building to an actual fight. "It's your own time you're wasting," Ms. Kruger said in her infuriating singsong voice. Even though I couldn't see her face, I knew she was standing there with her head slightly tilted, her chin slightly up, wearing an air of patience that said, I can do this all day. And we all knew it. The hubbub eventually died down. "Aaaaaand—thank you." A brittle quiet descended. "Now, on to the formalities," as though everyone had stopped talking the minute she asked them to. "Please join me in welcoming to the stage your Class President and spokesperson, Amy Middleton."

What? That's me! In all the drama about Leo, the photo, the goat, and our escape to the secret backstage hideout, I'd forgotten I was supposed to do a presentation! So had the others, if they even knew in the first place, which they probably didn't. Leo and Vanessa whipped around and stared at me. Vanessa nudged the door open a little more.

"Well, go on then."

"Are you crazy?" I whispered back. I could already hear a rumble of snickering giggles. Vanessa pushed me forward into the gap, and I could see that the curtains were pulled all the way around the room and across the terrace doors, so the whole place felt like a theater. Ms. Kruger in her wine-red sack—no better from a distance—lumbered down from the stage. The spotlight hovered there, on an empty circle of wavy curtain backdrop, the exact spot where for about ten years I had pictured myself beaming and fabulous in front of the whole school.

The rumble of giggling changed key into a kind of whispery, shifting anxiety as people started looking around, asking where I was, and the blood rushed to my face. I knew where I was, and in a horrible reversal of my long-cherished dream, the last place I wanted to be was out there in front of everyone. Second-to-last place was right here with Vanessa actually pushing me in the back.

"Get out there!" she insisted. "It's your chance to show them what you're really made of!"

What I'm really made of. What is that anyway? Blood and guts? Goat blood and guts? Pink chiffon? Up until a few hours before, I would have confidently answered that I am made of steel with a feathery spray of sequin, I am woman, I am strong, I am everyone's best friend, I am smart, I can run, and I am all about success and doing really well and I'm going to totally seal the deal of my own fabulousness by kissing Leo tonight. And now, I was huddling all smelly in an even smellier corridor, quite firmly convinced that the only good thing I'd ever done was pretend that a dead goat was a celebratory cake. And now I could see Gabby! Gabby, my former best friend, the girl who had been by my side all these years but secretly all the while hated me with a jealous passion, the one who started my night on the road to ruin, was right there, still looking rather lovely in the green halter-neck. As of course she would, because I chose it. She stood up and glided between the tables toward the stage, light glancing off her perfectly clean shoulders, at just the right pace between slow and fast, making people turn their heads as she went, head held high. Hang on! Those are my heads! That's my spotlight! What am I made of? I'm made of stuff that may be wrong, brash, dominating, and nonbiodegradable. Whatever it is, it won't be ignored.

"Hi everyone," Gabby breathed, half into and half out of the microphone, so it sounded like she was running toward us down a tunnel. "Welcome to the Graduating Class."

That was the cue. The lights dimmed, a picture flicked onto the screen behind her, and music swelled. But something was wrong. It wasn't the picture of the front of the school, taken on a particularly golden morning on a Sunday to avoid having any cars parked in front of it. One that I'd carefully selected from a folder of over fifty of them—you might as well have all of these, Ms. Kruger said. No. There was some terrible mistake because the whole ballroom was looking at a photo of me and Gabby in Year 7, hugging each other at the school swimming carnival, with stripes of colored paint on our faces to support our team. Blue. Painted like sports fanatics because we were only twelve at the time and didn't know that was uncool.

**Group Chat: Crystal, Tallulah, Jasi, Sumaya, Bianca, Kate**
**Friday, April 14, 8 p.m.**

**Crystal:** Wtf is this?

**Bianca:** I don't know

**Kate:** Gabby must have changed it

**Jasi:** Why?

**Crystal:** She's clearly lost the plot

**Tallulah:** Gabby took the pic, sent it to everyone

**Sumaya:** This is just weird

**Tallulah:** Bianca sent it to me

**Bianca:** Gabby didn't send me anything—I got it from someone else. Also I only sent it to you so that you would know what's going on

**Kate:** Yeah I don't know who took the pic

**Bianca:** Also I know you forwarded the pic, Tallulah

**Tallulah:** No I didn't I only sent it to Crystal

**Crystal:** I'd never forward something like that

**Sumaya:** I never got sent anything but all the boys did

**Jasi:** It's supposed to be Amy's presentation

**Crystal:** She's already presented everything she's got

SCHOOL COMMUNITY NEWSLETTER

## FROM THE PRINCIPAL'S DESK

As soon as the presentation began and I became aware that the pictures on display were *not* those from the preapproved slideshow, I immediately approached the sound desk and endeavored to rectify the situation. I did everything possible, even to the point of enlisting some of the students at a nearby table to help, and I would like to take this opportunity to thank Remy Velazquez, who is very proficient with such things and has always handled audiovisual issues excellently here at the school. However, the sound and light desk at the hotel ballroom was a different brand from ours, foreign to all of us and specifically designed to make it impossible for those unfamiliar with it to do anything at all. Also we were overtaken by events that distracted both myself and the professional tech assistant, and for some of this time the lights were all out.

**Chris Butt's Incident Report**

The presentation started and it was flicking through pictures that must have been different from what I saw before but I didn't think anything of it really at first because not my job. It's their business and I've been here for all sorts including religious things so if I stopped things every time weird stuff came up I wouldn't be doing my job properly. I'm trained to tune it out and just pay attention to the levels and stuff like that, I don't judge. So I was actually a bit surprised when the principal came up to me and started pressing buttons, she pushed me right out of the way and that's not procedure and it's not safe, and I told her as much. But she was panicking and I wasn't going to use physical force or anything, but that's when I realized the green-dress girl must of seriously messed around with things and then that's when stuff got really weird.

## AMY'S JOURNAL

The horrifying slideshow went on with its retrospective of me and Gabby being absolutely ridiculous together. Six years of goofy, embarrassing moments made all the worse by the fact that I didn't realize how embarrassing they were at the time. Painting each other's toenails, doing each other's hair, dressing up as horribly misconceived versions of rock stars, supermodels, bunny rabbits, and ballerinas. Hugging, smiling, grinning, grimacing, ugly crying, and ugly laughing. It was us.

"Unfortunately Amy isn't here to—" Gabby began again.

"Yes I am!" I bellowed in the deepest, most public-speakery voice I've ever produced, and before I knew what I was doing, I was carving my way between the tables, striding manfully through the ballroom. Which of course was quite easy to do now because I was barefoot and my mermaid skirt was torn at the knee. But where Gabby had crossed the room in a sea of derisive looks and knowing winks and shifting and at least half the room hardly caring, checking their phones or eating fries off other people's plates, when I did it, the world stopped moving. Jaws dropped. Silence. Gabby's jaw dropped too when she saw me coming, and she scuttled down the other side of the stage before I even got there. But the closer I got, the less confident I felt. The atmosphere was thick, the room seemed to be closing in on me, and I had to work really hard just to stay upright and breathe right now, as though I was drowning. I clung to the only thing that made sense. The last remaining shred of the plan for the perfect night that had not yet been completely ruined. The presentation. All the froth and bubble of my brain was just like waves and spray over rocks. The rock was the presentation speech. I'd carved that speech out, I'd laid it so firmly in my mind that nothing was going to wash it away. I faced the crowd, ready to deliver.

## Elizabeth Starkey's Statement to Police

When Amy Middleton walked up onto the stage, I could see that she had actually come through a staff-only service entrance at the back of the ballroom that was off-limits to the students. From where I was standing, I could see that there was another student there too, hiding just behind the door. This is a very serious matter. Ms. Kruger had told all of us in that initial email about supervision at the ball that the students had to stay in the foyer and the ballroom and they weren't allowed to wander anywhere else. She was very firm about this. One of the main reasons the staff had to be there was to make sure students didn't wander off. As I didn't want to cause any further disruption, I went to the service entrance very quietly to discipline the student and return them to where they were supposed to be. Obviously coming back out through the service entrance again would have been even more disruptive, so I ushered the student back down the service corridor and we exited at the first available door, which happened to open onto the terrace. I was trying to be as quick and quiet about it as possible so they wouldn't disturb the presentation any more than they already had. This is probably why I didn't notice anyone or anything else in the corridor. I just saw Leo Prince.

12

# AMY'S JOURNAL

"Principal Kruger." My voice sounded so in control, so commanding, so very grown-up that it didn't even sound like me. This is how you talk into a microphone, Gabby. "Teachers. Fellow students. Friends." My eyes swept over the ballroom, which I had brought to a complete standstill. All faces were turned toward me, and nothing moved, except for Ms. Kruger, a small, lumpy figure in a wine-red sack dress motoring toward the tech desk.

"What's going on here?" she trumpeted at the tech guy, at which point I became aware that the silence in the room had morphed into a steady flicker of giggles and a rising stream of hissing. Not hissing. Pissing. They were making pissing noises. At me.

"That is not the correct slideshow," barked Ms. Kruger from the tech desk as she pushed the guy out of the way and started pressing things, which brought the music to an abrupt halt, at which time the hissing sound reached a crescendo like we were in the middle of some terrible cicada-infested jungle.

"What is this?" shrieked Ms. Kruger. "Really, people, you are being very rude!"

"It's all right, Ms. Kruger." I spoke calmly. She had raised her voice, but I had a microphone. The hissing and pissing was breaking up into more pronounced clusters of giggles. "They're just doing it because . . . because . . ." I knew why they were doing it, they knew why they were doing it, did it need to be said? Just for the benefit of the clueless adults? But Ms. Kruger kept batting at the console, and the tech guy was now standing back with his hands splayed out to indicate his complete abdication of responsibility for anything that might happen ever.

"You touch the desk, it's not my problem," I heard him say over the rumble of ongoing pissing and snickering. It rose and fell, and I could see some eyes were distracted by the ongoing slideshow behind me. I turned around to face a pouting selfie, followed by a back-of-the-head hair-check shot, followed by a random puppy tied up in front of a supermarket, followed by a quick succession of three different kinds of shampoo. None of them good. I've already told you, Gabby, you can't get good shampoo at the supermarket.

"Make that STOP," shrieked Ms. Kruger, as she smacked at the laptop attached to the tech desk. The slideshow froze on the ugliest ugly selfie ever of Gabby, right up the nose and everything. The room exploded in jeers and laughter that was way uglier than the selfie.

"Oh, SHUT UP!" I spat into the microphone. So loud that the speakers cracked and the whole room fell into a collective gasp of shock. A few nervous giggles punctuated the silence.

Normally I would cringe and smile and try to make everyone feel comfortable again, because we all hate awkwardness, especially me, but we were way past that now. Even Ms. Kruger and the tech guy stared at me. Everyone was staring at me. In a terrible twist, I realized this was exactly how I'd always imagined this moment, except that people would be admiring instead of staring with a mixture of horror and derision and—what else? Scorn?

"Show us your tits," someone called out from the back, in a deliberately distorted voice meant to show irony, but still just as effective in pointing out to everyone that I was now nothing more than a joke. The room erupted into giggles again so you could hardly hear Ms. Kruger.

"Who said that?" she snapped as she scanned the back of the room, but the laughter continued.

Blood surged to my cheeks. How dare they. How dare my classmates—this grinning bunch of fools—laugh at me? But their laughter gave way to a ripple of uncertainty, and I could see the fear. Fear that they too were actually just one little mistake, one quirky twist of events away from being a laughingstock themselves. They were all following each other, finding safety in the crowd, but the way was precarious and narrow. There was not enough room for everyone, nobody was safe from being pushed out or off. How inhibited they all were, only daring to be individual in the same way as everyone else. How careful they were to conceal their vulnerabilities. And here I was, quite literally a gaping wound, and the longer I stood there, the more vulnerable I became, and the more afraid they were from having to witness it. The poor things. They're not sheep, they're not goats; they're children, actually. We're all children. And the pageantry of a ball was not the thing that would release us into adulthood. Certainly not the kind of adulthood that means anything.

I reached down to the edges of the black sweater and lifted it up over my head. Held it away from my face and hair by habit—my makeup and curls had long ago been destroyed by rubbing, night air, and tears. I could hear a murmur of consternation, "Oh, *Amy*!" from Ms. Kruger as I lifted up my sweater, as though I were about to take it all off. Not that it would matter at this point if anyone saw my tits. They'd already seen everything else. I flung the sweater to the floor—maybe with a hint of drama. I'm not stupid; I know how to milk a good moment. It's part of the story, and it stopped Ms. Kruger in her tracks. I stood there in my dress, ruined with rips and mud and bloodstains. A map of my disgrace. That's what they thought they wanted. More evidence to set me apart. Something more they could laugh at. And they did, they laughed. The whole crowd went berserk with hooting and laughter and a flurry of people taking pictures, and standing up to get better pictures, and running up closer to get the best ever picture of my complete humiliation.

"So this is it?" They hardly heard me. They were all having too much fun, laughing and yelping and taking photos and videos with their stupid cameras. But I still had the microphone. "This is your school ball. The only one you're going to get." They could hardly hear me. "Is this how you want it to be?" Somehow, I was floating outside of it, and nothing could hurt me anymore. It was all just so silly. The makeup, the hair, the suits. I had thought we would be different if we put it all on. But it didn't change anything. We were still in the schoolyard, dressed up in silly costumes.

"This was our chance, our moment to show each other and our teachers and parents who we really are," I said quietly. Into the microphone. "And I guess this is it. This is who we are. Who I am. What you want me to be. And this is YOU."

The jeering faded. "I mean, come on. Is this really the moment you want to remember?" The cameras dropped, one by one.

Silence. I held my head higher. I could barely believe it. Had I made an impact? Had I actually gotten through to them, after everything, not with some well-chosen words of dignified encouragement, but by reflecting back at them their own fragility? The most glorious feeling of triumph welled in me.

"You don't need this." I was smiling gently now, like a benevolent monarch. "I don't need this. What we all need is—"

I believe I was going to say love, or perhaps kindness, but we'll never know, because at that moment I was hit in the head by a flying toilet-paper roll.

"Shit tickets!" yelled Macca, and the entire ballroom erupted in jeering again, but ten times louder this time.

"All right, that's enough," roared Ms. Kruger. She bent over the desk and hit another button, restarting the slideshow, this time accompanied by a blaring disco pop beat that whipped the crowd into an apocalyptic frenzy of shrieking, laughing, and dancing on chairs that went from zero to a hundred in a second, then just as quickly collapsed into chaos with a sudden *BANG*.

A crashing door, and a familiar figure in black with a scrape of long black hair flew backward into the ballroom, apparently projected or pushed, or at the very least pursued by a squeaky cart draped with a very familiar tablecloth. Oh no. Vanessa fell backward on her bum and knocked Amberley Minetti off her chair completely, sending two empty plates and assorted cutlery crashing to the floor.

## Tony Gambino's Incident Report

I work in Services and Maintenance. I was on shift that night. I saw a girl in the service corridor that shouldn't of been there. I asked her what she was doing. She told me to leave her the F alone. She pushed a cart at me. I took the cart. She took it back. She kept swearing. She said shed F-ing report me. I let go the cart. She went through the door into the Chandeleer Room. I went back to work. I don't know what happend after that.

**Vanessa Nguyen's letter to the manager of the Pacific Crest Hotel**

*When Amy Middleton entered the ballroom, I observed that a member of school staff spotted our hideout. I duly retreated with the cart and urged my remaining coconspirator to do the same, but he did not. Before he could close the door, the teacher reached it, entered the service corridor, seized him, and ushered him away in the opposite direction from me and out the next door, which I later discovered led to the terrace. Relieved that the goat still remained undetected, I continued to wait quietly alone but was soon accosted by another hotel employee, whom I believe is known to you. There is no doubt in my mind that this employee was either deliberately trying to cause trouble for Elroy or engaged in some kind of nefarious frolic of his own, as Elroy had taken pains to sequester us in a secluded space off-limits to ordinary staff. This person discovered me when he crossed the passageway at the other end of our hiding place, apparently on the lookout for something or someone. If he had not been actively seeking, my presence would have been undetected as I was silent and immobile in the darkness. However, he did see me and immediately approached in an intimidating manner even though I was clearly neither fleeing nor posing a threat. In point of fact, I was vulnerable and helpless, being less than 110 lbs, trapped in a foreign environment, and this person was comfortable in this space and physically very dominating. He threatened me and abused me when I refused to comply with his demands to accompany him. I felt extremely unsafe and struck out to protect myself as this person behaved in a manner toward me that was insulting and aggressive, not at all professional, and I had serious cause to suspect the legitimacy of his intentions. He placed his hands on me and attempted to remove me from the corridor by force. I resisted, as is my right. He continued to apply force to me and to the cart, which I placed in between us in order to prevent him from placing his hands on my body. In my attempts to resist, I leaned all my weight against the door into the ballroom, while this person in turn used all his strength to pull the cart and me, against my will, toward himself. The door opened as I leaned against it, and when this person let go of the cart, I flew backward into the room, stumbled, fell over, and bruised my right thigh. I was unable to maintain control of the cart as it went flying into the room, with the consequence that the goat ended up contaminating I don't know how many people and surfaces. I believe this person let go of the cart at that moment precisely because he intended this outcome. I, however, was doing everything in my power to prevent it and keep myself and the goat safe.*

## AMY'S JOURNAL

The cart skittered and bumped between the tables, picking up speed as people pushed it away from them, until it crashed into the stage at my feet with the force of a small train. The tablecloth caught under the wheel at some point, the impact sent it flying off, and the body of the goat slid right off the cart, missing my feet by the length of its hair. It flew across the stage and smashed into the base of the projector screen, then bounced back, while the screen wobbled and swayed backward and sideways, and the goat, now a splayed and mangled mess of fur and hooves and horns, with one leg sticking up in a really grisly unnatural way, gleamed in the spotlight. The entire room gasped in horror, then was plunged into sudden darkness, almost as though the force of our breaths had actually turned out the lights. Ms. Kruger was flailing at every button on the tech desk, and possibly swearing, but the parade of Gabby's photo roll continued: watching-TV selfie, her dog looking out the window, a flower in the park, another selfie, another selfie—all a bit distorted on the wobbling screen, which tipped and lurched like a sinking ship, and then, amid little theatrical screams, an almighty crash signaled its final demise as it plunged to the floor, taking with it part of the curtain, which then proceeded to come off its tracks along the entire length of the terrace windows.

SCHOOL COMMUNITY NEWSLETTER

FROM THE PRINCIPAL'S DESK

It was during the "blackout" stage that the screen fell. It did *not* fall in the vicinity of any students or any of the dining tables and it didn't hit anyone. Even if it had, by the time it hit the floor, it was falling quite slowly, and although bulky, the projection screen is not heavy and at no time was anyone's life in danger. I believe the curtains were ripped off their tracks not by the weight of the screen but by a process of "unhooking" whereby the corner of the screen unhooked the curtain off its track and then the weight of the curtain itself brought the whole thing down. Once again, the curtain did not fall on anybody nor did it fall close to anybody, and yes, the curtains are heavy but not at all heavy enough to cause suffocation.

# AMY'S JOURNAL

So we could all see straight out to the terrace garden, which I thought would be forever branded as my toilet, but teenage attention spans are short. Now it was a romantic love scene starring . . . Leo and Miss Starkey! The entire ballroom froze. Eyes and mouths gaped open. The two lovers were surrounded by fairy lights, heads haloed in gold, as she tenderly leaned in to kiss him and he deflected her advance, and then she pushed back, raised her hand, and slapped him with so much force that his whole body braced against it and for a split second he looked as though he might hit her back!

13

**Chat: Macca, Fred**
**Friday, April 14, 8:10 p.m.**

**Fred:** Did she just slap him?

**Macca:** Nah he dodged it—I think she hit his arm? Crazy tho

**Chat: Bianca, Kate**
**Friday, April 14, 8:10 p.m.**

**Kate:** It sort of looked like he was swatting away a fly or something

**Bianca:** Tallulah said she saw a slap

**Group Chat: Crystal, Tallulah, Jasi, Sumaya**
**Friday, April 14, 8:10 p.m.**

**Tallulah:** I got a video of the whole thing

**Sumaya:** Holy shit—even the slap?

**Jasi:** Wasn't a slap, was it? He ducked?

**Crystal:** Not from where I'm sitting—she made contact

**Chat: Tallulah, Bianca**
**Friday, April 14, 8:15 p.m.**

**Tallulah:** Here's the vid

**Bianca:** Can barely see anything!

**Tallulah:** I still reckon she slapped him tho

**Group Chat: Crystal, Tallulah, Jasi, Sumaya**
**Friday, April 14, 8:15 p.m.**

**Sumaya:** Shit

**Jasi:** I'll never cheat on a math test again

**Crystal:** You might not have to. She's a goner for sure

## Dev Khoury's Statement to the Police

Before I say what I saw, I want to assure you that my statement is not biased. Other students from the school maybe have told you that I got the top mark in Math in Year 11 with Miss Starkey as my teacher. You should also know that Leo called me a slur in Year 8 because I won dodgeball against him in PE. (I stayed at the back of the gym and collected all the balls and passed them up to the people on the front line, until I was the last one standing. Leo said that was cheating and called me the aforementioned slur, but I won fair and square.) But I am putting these biases aside to accurately recount what I saw. I was late to the ballroom dinner, and someone had taken my seat at my assigned table at the back of the ballroom. Even if I had been on time, the seating plan was a mess since a bunch of the guys didn't book their tables early enough in the year to ensure they were all sitting together, so they completely ignored the plan and took over two tables, leaving a number of people without an assigned seat. Luckily for me, Jason Galanis let me sit at his table, which was close to the front of the stage. The big glass doors from the ballroom to the terrace had been closed and draped with curtains so that the presentation could start, but there is another door onto the terrace from the service hallway, which is how Miss Starkey and Leo got out there. I've drawn a map, if it's of any use to you—my cousin had her wedding reception at this ballroom, and I know how confusing the layout is if you've never been there before. When the curtains came down, I could clearly see Miss Starkey and Leo standing on the terrace, especially because of the blackout, and the terrace was lit up with fairy lights. Miss Starkey was yelling something at Leo, but I couldn't hear the exact words through the glass. He said something back, at which point I saw Miss Starkey slap Leo on his cheek. He definitely dodged a little bit, and looked murderous afterward, but she still hit him. I saw it.

---

***Transcription of Detective Wozniak's interview with Leo Prince***

**SW:** So how did you end up with Miss Starkey on the terrace?

**LEO:** I was at the ball, she was at the ball, she took me outside to yell at me. Like I said.

**SW:** Why?

**LEO:** She was mad, I dunno. I was . . . doing the wrong thing or something. She caught me hiding with the freaking goat.

**SW:** And the others.

**LEO:** Yes.

**SW:** So why did she just take you?

**LEO:** Oh. Well . . . um . . . Amy was . . . she actually wasn't there because she went up to give her speech.

**SW:** So where was Vanessa?

**LEO:** Um . . . I'm not sure.

**SW:** Weren't you with her? And the goat?

**LEO:** No. Yes. Yes I was.

**SW:** So why did Miss Starkey just take you?

**LEO:** I don't know . . . I . . . I took her car. Didn't I? She was really mad about that. So . . .

**SW:** How did she know? At that point?

**LEO:** Pardon?

**SW:** How did she know you took her car? If you just secretly took it, and then brought it back and met up with your friends, how did she find out?

*(pause)*

**LEO:** Couldn't tell you.

**SW:** She didn't say?

**LEO:** She must have seen me. Or something. I don't know.

**SW:** And that's why she yelled at you?

**LEO:** Yeah.

**SW:** What did she say?

**LEO:** I don't remember! Probably, "You took my car, you shouldn't have done that, why did you do that?" I don't know. She said what teachers say. I didn't really pay attention. I mean, I didn't care. It was all fine, the car was fine.

**SW:** You know a lot of people saw this.

**LEO:** I know. So? They would have seen that she was just mad. Whatever.

**SW:** Did she hit you?

**LEO:** She tried.

**SW:** Why would she do that?

**LEO:** I guess . . . I don't know. Maybe she really loves that car.

## Elizabeth Starkey's Statement to Police

He was very rude and aggressive. I said that he had to return to the ballroom with everyone else and he said something like, "You can't tell me what to do." I'm certain that's exactly what he said. I said, "Get back in there right now," and he then called me something I can't repeat here. It starts with a C. I was brought up in a very conservative Catholic environment so I was very offended by his use of this word. That is why I unfortunately lost my temper a little bit and raised my hand toward him. It was never a serious hit and he deflected easily. I would never do such a thing except under extreme provocation. Anyone who knows me would agree.

SCHOOL COMMUNITY NEWSLETTER

## FROM THE PRINCIPAL'S DESK

As the room was very dark at that point, apart from the spotlight on the stage, when the curtains came down everyone in the ballroom was clearly able to see the lighted terrace beyond the glass doors. I had a very good view myself so I am able to say with great certainty what could be seen and heard from within the ballroom. I do wear glasses but they are for reading only and I have excellent vision of what goes on in the middle distance, as the terrace then was. I can confirm that there was a student on the terrace with a teaching staff member and they appeared to be in a conversation and the staff member raised their hand in a gesture that would be consistent with what one might call a slap. The staff member then became aware that they could be seen and entered the ballroom at the same time that the lights came back on. They did not say anything at this point but just walked straight through the ballroom to the exit. The identity of the teacher is not a subject of speculation. You can rest assured that those who are directly affected by this matter are fully aware. Please refrain from gossiping; it does no one any good.

## Elizabeth Starkey's Statement to Police

I decided to leave the situation and went back into the ballroom via the terrace doors. The lights were all out so I didn't realize that the presentation was still going on. The lights came back on just as I walked in. I headed straight through the ballroom toward the main doors because I felt unwell again. I wasn't running away. I walked. Everyone who was there would have seen that. And I didn't even have my handbag, it was still on the table. I just wanted to clear my head a little.

## AMY'S JOURNAL

She stormed into the ballroom, through the terrace glass doors, just as the lights came back on, and the entire cohort's gaze of horror was now on her. Which she brushed off because she probably didn't even feel it, either because she had no idea we'd all just witnessed the moment, or because that's the kind of despicable person she is.

"Excuse me," she appeared to say lightly as she stalked her way through the room between the tables, straight for the exit, head held high.

## Chris Butt's Incident Report

I don't even know what happened but next thing you know the lights are off and the screen's come down and everything's gone quiet and the lights come back on again and this other female person is walking straight through the ballroom and the principal just turns to me and she says like really stern, "Bring her back to me," like she suddenly turned into some scary assassin from a movie or something and I will never understand why I did this right then but I did as I was told. I followed that woman, I left the desk, which I know is the number one thing in procedure that you must never do but believe me there is no way I would have done it if it weren't very much emergency extenuating circumstances. Like the way the principal spoke to me it was like that woman had a bomb.

SCHOOL COMMUNITY NEWSLETTER

FROM THE PRINCIPAL'S DESK

I directed our tech support person to follow and bring the teacher back to me. This is why the technical support person was then not in attendance in the period that immediately followed.

## AMY'S JOURNAL

Ms. Kruger said something to the tech guy, and he lumbered off after Miss Starkey. Ms. Kruger slapped at the laptop again, the music abruptly stopped—and the slideshow froze. On that photo. THAT photo. A wavy wobbly version of it, projected now onto curtain rather than a screen, but still the photo. Still very recognizable. All of it. A rumble of suppressed laughter, mingled with shock and discomfort and general unrest, rippled around the room. Nobody knew what to think anymore, let alone what reaction would be the quickest route back to normal. Surely after this, there could be no normal. I couldn't do anything about the picture now. It was projected, I couldn't block it, I'd only become another screen for it. Gabby charged to the tech desk as Ms. Kruger charged toward me.

SCHOOL COMMUNITY NEWSLETTER

## FROM THE PRINCIPAL'S DESK

I personally was unaware of the nature of the photograph that was then projected and that remained frozen on the wall for a period of several minutes. While, as stated, my middle-distance vision is excellent, I was occupied with unfolding events and endeavoring to take control of the situation. Also the projection was not onto the screen, but onto the back curtain of the ballroom, which had remained intact, as only the side curtain on the wall to the terrace was affected by the screen's fall. As the photograph was projected onto the curtain, it was not a very clear image; it was wavy and the colors were somewhat muted, which also prevented me from immediately identifying the image. I believe most of the staff were unaware of what it was, and potentially some of the more innocent members of the student cohort as well. I believe that most who immediately recognized it only did so because they had already seen it. I therefore can confidently assert that most of the damage done by the public display of this photo was already done *before* it was projected, and the remaining damage was very much mitigated by its blurriness.

## AMY'S JOURNAL

"Stop it, stop it now, really! Control yourselves people!" Ms. Kruger bellowed.

I stepped sideways over Choc-Top. Ms. Kruger lunged for the microphone as I shouted into it, "Turn it off!" But no one did anything. "Remy? Please!" I begged as Ms. Kruger seized the microphone. But Remy Velazquez just stood next to the tech desk with his arms folded, clearly enjoying the spectacle along with everyone else, waiting to see what our principal would say while standing next to a projection of a vulva that was almost as tall as her. (I'm exaggerating. But not by much.)

Expectant silence.

"This is a ball, you're in a ballroom," declared Ms. Kruger. "Not a zoo. Next year it'll be the gym, and that's a promise. You've ruined it for the Year Elevens." The horrified silence erupted into giggles and I couldn't help it either, even I cracked a smile. She stared down at poor Choc-Top with a look of revulsion.

"Who is responsible for this?" She swept out an arm gesture that took in the goat, the ruined screen, me, and everyone else.

Silence.

"Amy?" Ms. Kruger turned on me with a harsh look of judgment and dislike. The kind of look teachers give out regularly to the bad kids, but never, ever to me. "What have you done?"

"Nothing, Miss," said Vanessa as she pulled herself up from among the tables and raised her hand. "It was me," she announced, with just the right amount of sacrificial drama. That was when the emotional roller coaster of My Journey With Vanessa reached its end point: I like the girl. No, I don't just like her; I love her. She is actually very much the best.

"No, Miss, it was me, actually." Dev raised his hand as he stepped out from where he was leaning in the doorway with a plate of chips. I liked him already.

"No, it was actually me," said Gabby, from the tech desk.

Leo raised his hand from the doorway onto the terrace. "But it was all my fault, really."

"I killed it," I said.

Then a weird thing happened. Bianca stood up.

"I forwarded the photo," she confessed.

Then Macca stood up. "So did I."

"Me too."

"I popped the balloons."

"So did I."

"I laughed."

"It was me."

"I made it a meme."

"I'm sorry Amy."

"It isn't your fault, Amy."

"It's my fault!"

"WE LOVE YOU, AMY!"

For one hot second, I felt the love. The understanding that whatever happened that night, I was still a person, worthy of dignity and respect. That it had happened to all of us. We were a community, we shared responsibility, we acknowledged group complicity, we would leave no one behind. It was quite stunning, for the few seconds it lasted.

Then Macca, who had run to the side of the stage in the momentary lull, shook the curtain so the picture wobbled, and yelled out, "It's moving! It's gonna eat us alive!"

And someone else yelled, "ATTACK OF THE KILLER COOCH!"

And the room erupted in laughter and all the phones came out to video Ms. Kruger and me swimming in the ripples of light.

## Elizabeth Starkey's Statement to Police

In the lower foyer, while I was just walking very calmly toward the front door of the hotel, an overweight man in a black T-shirt whom I had never met before grabbed hold of my arm and demanded that I come with him. I had no idea who this man was, I'd never seen him before in my life. Of course I resisted. I believe this is assault, to touch a person without their consent, and he left quite a bruise on my arm. I have photos to prove it. The man eventually told me that Ms. Kruger wanted to see me, and when he said that, of course I accompanied him back up to the ballroom.

## Chris Butt's Incident Report

I followed the female out of the ballroom and down the stairs, she was going at a fair pace too, and she realized I was following her so she stepped it up but I called after her, she was deliberately ignoring me and I had to grab her arm eventually and then she kicked up all this drama and tried to make me out to be some kind of harasser, which is absolute bullshit. The whole night I followed procedure and endeavored to satisfy the hirer. I think I went above and beyond to be honest, and the whole thing got cocked up by that girl in green.

I'm happy to answer any more questions about it but I've said my piece.

## AMY'S JOURNAL

"QUIET!" bellowed Ms. Kruger. She turned to me in confusion. What on earth was going on? Then she saw the curtain behind, and the projected picture. Still there. Still pissing. She frowned. She squinted. "What's that of, then?" And I watched the realization spread over her face like a new dawn. She gasped in horror. Her first instinct was to stand in front of it and cover it with her body, but the wine-red sack made an even better screen. Oh god. "Get it OFF, Remy! Gabby! Anyone!" she bellowed.

"I'm trying! It's frozen!" whined Gabby from the tech desk. She desperately flicked at various switches, finally got us an error message and a wheel of death, then plunged the whole room into disco mode with thumping music and whirling colored lights that wiped out the picture and any sense of propriety. The room exploded in whooping and shrieking, everyone stood up to rush the dance floor, and those who didn't have room danced on chairs and tables.

Ms. Kruger stared at me helplessly.

"What in god's name is happening?" she asked me, with the blank gray face of someone facing utter ruin. I knew that look. But I had moved beyond it. I just shrugged. I almost laughed, she looked so funny, but the music was so loud now that there was barely room in my head for anything else. I stepped from side to side to the beat. Before I knew it, my hips were swinging, my bloody hands were in the air, and I was dancing. Right there, on the stage, in a torn and bloodied evening gown, flooded with whirling lights, trying not to step on Choc-Top, dancing like no one was watching, right along with everyone else. But I caught Ms. Kruger's look of despair as she scanned the heaving room, and I saw her face harden as she saw the tech guy emerge in the doorway, dragging a very grumpy-looking Miss Starkey.

14

## Elizabeth Starkey's Statement to Police

I went back to the ballroom and spoke to Ms. Kruger and Ben Chang (assistant principal). They just wanted to know what happened with Leo and I told them. I didn't mention at the time that I'd spent an hour outside feeling sick, as I didn't feel comfortable discussing my personal health situation in front of a man. I said that I had spent the entire evening in the ballroom, which was not true, but really as I wasn't being paid to supervise the event, it was none of their business where I had been anyway, and I was actually doing them a favor. Ms. Kruger said she would need to talk further with me and Leo, and I said of course that was fine but I really wanted to go home. She said I could go, so I got my handbag and went straight to the parking lot and drove home alone.

I regret that the evening went so badly for the school but I don't believe any of it was my fault. I wasn't even there for most of the night and for the part that I was there, I was doing my job. I didn't actually see the presentation. Of course I'm sorry that I tried to slap a student, but I never really hit him anyway and he wasn't hurt. In fact because he deflected me away with quite a lot of force, if anyone was hurt it was me. And I was definitely hurt by the tech person who practically tackled me in the hotel's lower foyer. I'm only slight so that really wasn't necessary. The people at the front desk can back me up, they would have seen the whole thing.

I don't know who took my car out while I was at the ball, or if anyone took it out at all. There are quite a few girls in that student cohort who are malicious and gossipy. There are some others who may be upset with me because I am a very strict teacher, and also possibly because they are jealous. They might be making up stories just to get back at me, which is very unfair as I have done nothing to them except do my job.

I just want to finish by repeating that I didn't hit Leo Prince. I've never hit a student in my life and I'm not going to start now.

The staff member in question has been suspended pending further investigation.

No school students, staff, or hotel staff were seriously injured at the ball. We had a Safety Officer on duty at the time (Health and PE department head Martin Kreiwoldt) who provided ice for a couple of turned ankles, which quite frankly were the result of students wearing inappropriate footwear and/or not paying enough attention on the stairs. While there was a lot of blood observed, it was for the most part dry (not pooling, gushing, dripping, or spraying as many have reported) and none of it belonged to ANY PERSON in attendance at the ball that night.

The circumstances leading to the incident either were remote and unforeseeable or were deliberately and maliciously orchestrated against school policy. We believe the school was as best prepared as possible under the circumstances. Please ONLY call Kimmbalee if you have further questions AFTER you have read this account THOROUGHLY.

# AMY'S JOURNAL

The dance floor was going off. I felt drunk. The lights made everything colorful and dim, the music was so loud I could feel it thumping through my body, and the roller coaster of the last few hours had left me lightheaded and somehow invincible. I danced. I danced like a wild thing, shimmied like a silly salmon, rocked out like a boss. With everyone. Even people who I don't normally hang out with. Especially people I don't normally hang out with. Macca, Crystal, Hyun Jae, Mischa, Danielle, Vanessa, Dev. Bianca and Kate were dancing and crying and laughing simultaneously. I actually had to tell them to calm down, they looked so much like they were on drugs. They hugged me and apologized and I had to just say, forget about it. Like, for real. Let's just live tonight, in this totally fucked-up version of a party where I look like absolute shit and I somehow feel like queen of the night precisely because everyone else has acted abominably. Yes. That's it. I am the living expression of everyone else's failure to act like a decent human being, but I'm still dancing. Turns out that a world ruled by social media anarchy is just like a high-stakes version of the kindergarten game Opposite Day.

And there, in my peripheral vision, was Gabby. Watching mostly, not on the dance floor. Nobody was talking to her much. Kate and Bianca are very good at forgetting things—everything from the time a movie starts to the quadratic formula—and it's the most infuriating thing about them, but also quite handy. They'll never stay mad at you for long. I can sit and wallow and fume for days, but they will literally have completely forgotten what the problem was by the time their favorite fashion vlogger posts a new video. But Gabby's a bit more like me. So I danced, with my scabby knees and filthy hands and torn dress, actually rather loving the drama of it all, to a certain extent—certainly there was no way I was going to leave the flattering lighting for the glare of the bathroom. Here, half in the dark, in the music, I was almost living out the night I thought it would be. Gabby still looked like she did when we left the house, but inside she was a total mess, I could tell. She sat on the edges, on her own, smiling in a rueful but slightly superior way, as though she had brought up this rowdy rabble of young people herself. Which she bloody hadn't.

Poor thing, though. From my spot on the dance floor, with the smug perspective of a very wise person who had been to hell and back, I could see that she had actually had a pretty shit night as well. She may not have displayed her bits, but everyone saw the stupidity of her photo album, and there's no denying it was hugely embarrassing. Worse, in a way, because it was more personally intimate. Lots of people have a vagina. But not everyone takes a snotty picture of themselves. Plus, she'd taken the photo of me, she'd shared it, and everyone knew. The vileness of the whole thing didn't start with me; it started with her. So when I saw her sitting all on her own, I actually felt a bit sorry for her. And I also actually felt a bit—yes, I can admit it here because this is my diary and I'd better not start lying to myself—victorious. Like I had won. She hurt me, and there was no doubt in my mind that it was at least partly out of jealousy. She wanted to bring me down. But I fought my way out of it, and in the end, I still got all the attention, and she was just on the sidelines. Which is where she always seems to end up, and I know she doesn't really like it.

I sashayed over and danced in front of her, and held out my arms to invite her onto the floor with me. She shook her head and batted me away with a smile. "Come on!" I tried to pull her out of her chair, but she pulled her hands back.

"I can't," she shouted over the music, stood up, and retreated toward the empty buffet outside. I followed in a dance walk.

"Come back!" I entreated. "You might as well."

"I can't."

"Yes you can."

"I don't want to."

"Yes you do!"

She smiled. I smiled. We do know each other, after all—we're BFFs. Like, for real. Then she looked like she was going to cry again.

"I didn't mean to ruin your night."

"Yes you did, but I forgive you."

"No, I didn't."

"It's okay. You hate me, because I'm just so much more fabulous than you."

"You *are* so much more fabulous than me."

"I know."

"That's why I love you."

"And I love you too, baby. Let's dance."

"No, but really."

"I know! Same."

"But. Really."

Oh no. How many revelations can there possibly be tonight?

"Really?" I asked again, more gently.

"Really. Yes. No. I don't know. I mean, I do love you and I also—maybe. Love you. Like, have a crush on you. Or something."

"Like—like in *that* way?"

"I don't know. I'm sorry. Forget I said anything."

"Are you serious right now?"

She just sighed, and looked at me, and seemed sad.

"I know you don't think of me in that way but it's okay, I don't mind. I never expected you to." She wiped a tear away.

"How long have you—"

She shrugged and twisted her mouth. So, forever. To be honest, I was kind of mad in that moment.

"I thought you were my friend!"

"I am! Please, Amy, don't hate me. I couldn't bear it."

"Why didn't you tell me?"

"I tried."

"No you didn't!"

Her eyes filled with tears, she stood awkwardly on one leg, and her gaze drifted to the ground.

"Remember the poem?"

"What poem?"

"Bevan's love letter poem?"

Bevan at that moment happened to be dancing on the stage, swinging his jacket above his head and doing the pelvic thrust. This is what happens to the socially challenged when they let loose.

"Bevan's love letter poem?" I echoed. Oh my god. Bevan's love letter. "That was you?"

"It's an acrostic," she said, with some hurt dignity. "I thought you'd get it."

My mind hurtled back, into what seemed like another time. *Giving up . . . A place in my heart . . . Believe . . . Because someday . . . Yours.* GABBY. How could I have missed that? I knew that first line was weird.

"You wrote that?"

"Yes. I know about acrostics. I can write poems." She was quivering with injury that I could feel as intensely as my own.

She was me. Rejected, hurt, nursing the wreckage of a cherished vision. I had become Leo, in the deserted function room. That's how it works. We're all each other, eventually, in a roundabout twisted way, all looking for that perfect moment that is never, ever going to work out the way you think it is.

"It's a really good poem," I assured her. "I see that now."

We hugged. And she felt like shit, and I felt like shit too, and we just existed in that new particular pile of weird, which might never have actually come out if it weren't for the rest of the craziness. I kissed her on the cheek.

"Does this mean everything is different?" she asked.

"I think . . . there's no point having a ball like this unless it actually changes things."

"So what will change?" she said with a sobbing little hiccup.

And I just shrugged, took her hand, and wiggled my shoulders and my hips along to the music until she laughed.

**Chat: LochNess, Devinitely**
**Friday, April 14, 8:45 p.m.**

**LochNess:** Do you have my black sweater?

**LochNess:** The one I gave Amy?

**Devinitely:** No why would I

**LochNess:** Did you see anyone take it?

**LochNess:** I can't find it

**Devinitely:** So

**LochNess:** Well I want it back

**Devinitely:** So talk to Amy then

**LochNess:** Ok

**Devinitely:** I mean why text me

**LochNess:** Maybe 'cause I'm sorry and can't admit it

**Devinitely:** 🙄

**LochNess:** I'm sorry, Dev

**LochNess:** I'm really sorry

**LochNess:** Forgive me?

**Devinitely:** You dragged me into helping you ruin something I actually wanted to go to and enjoy

**LochNess:** I'd argue that, despite my best efforts to ruin it, this has turned into the best school ball ever in the history of school balls

**LochNess:** But I am sorry

**LochNess:** You still had fun. You got to sit with Jason Galanis

**Devinitely:** Shut up

**LochNess:** :)

**Devinitely:** I will forgive you

**LochNess:** Finally!

**Devinitely:** After you call the goat's owners and say you killed their pet

**LochNess:** Ugh

**LochNess:** Ok

**Vanessa Nguyen's letter to the manager of the Pacific Crest Hotel**

*Certain other events impeded my progress but as soon as possible I approached Ms. Kruger for practical assistance. She directed me to an animal hospital that was able to send an ambulance to retrieve and dispose of the animal's corpse as per the appropriate legislation. Unfortunately the hospital is not centrally based and owing to the lateness of the hour, it took more than 90 minutes for the ambulance to arrive. This gave me ample time to fully confess my actions to school and hotel staff, discuss the ramifications, and reflect very seriously on my personal culpability. It was also incumbent upon me to call the goat's owner, impart the sad news of its passing, and inform my parents.*

## AMY'S JOURNAL

I wish it was easier to pick the right moment to leave the party. You'd think there'd be a huge identifiable period between euphoria (everyone happy, music pumping, fun, games, flirting, having the best time ever) and melancholy (everyone fake or kind of repulsive, music winding down, the realization that the journey from right here and now to being tucked up in bed is just going to be terrible). Yet it's so weird, you never can pinpoint that transition moment and get out before it's too late. So there I am on the dance floor, kind of still swaying, thinking oh my god they're never going to let me back in the limo, I'm going to have to call my parents, and then at some stage we're going to have to talk about what happened. Which I really, quite deeply, and profoundly never ever want to do.

I tried to will myself back into the party zone, but I couldn't. It was gone forever, much like my hopes and dreams of a perfect school ball. And then I saw him. Leo. Sitting at a table, flicking through his phone by himself, a picture of incredibly handsome, well-dressed misery.

I slid into a chair at his side.

"Hey."

"Hey."

His eyes flicked toward the doorway where Ms. Kruger was deep in discussion with Mr. Kreiwoldt. The worst kind of teacher discussion, confidential and serious, not the usual theatrical overreaction. There were going to be consequences. Leo tried to pretend he wasn't looking, but he couldn't hide it. They were talking about him and Miss Starkey. He knew it and I knew it.

"You're going to have to tell," I said.

"Tell what?"

"Or I will."

"Tell what?"

"You know what."

"Well, you don't know anything, so—"

"Doesn't matter, because it's true. Isn't it?"

He hung his head and looked at the blank face of his phone. He tossed it like it was a hand grenade he wanted to throw.

"I don't know what you're talking about. Anyway, there's nothing to say, because everything's fine now. I'm fine."

"No you're not."

"Yes I am."

"She took advantage of you, Leo."

"I said it's fine."

"No it's not. It's creepy, and it's wrong."

"I'm fine!"

"That's got nothing to do with it. She broke the law. There's a whole system designed to deal with exactly that."

He sighed, stretched back, ran a long-fingered hand through his curls, and met my eyes. I've never seen him look so lovely and so raw. And I realized that in all the terrible things that had happened to me that night, none of it was as bad as what had actually been done to him. Yes, they'd taken my image, but that was all. At that moment I knew that Miss Starkey had taken everything.

"It's not your fault."

"I'm not . . ." His voice drifted off.

"What?"

"I'm not ready."

I didn't know if the shine in his eyes was just their everyday glow, or if he was about to cry, but I knew I had to comfort this enormous, warm, and desperately sad handsome person. So I moved closer to him and I put my dirty, smelly, bloody arms around him and he put his clean suited arms around me and hugged me, like a boy who needs a hug, who appreciates someone who knows what he's going through and will do anything to support him through it. I lifted my face to him. He looked down at me. The lights spiraled around us. The music was romantic and slow and sexy. Our faces moved closer. I could feel his breath on my lips. And I knew, as deeply and thoroughly as I've ever known anything, that I could kiss him right now, and if I did, it would be really, really wrong.

So I didn't.

# 15

---

***Transcription of Detective Wozniak's interview with Leo Prince***

**SW:** Leo.

**LEO:** Look, can I go yet?

**SW:** I'm going to ask you directly.

**LEO:** It's almost—

**SW:** I will ask you this directly, Leo. Have you and Miss Starkey ever been involved sexually? Or romantically?

*(pause)*

**SW:** Leo? You're shaking your head. Does that mean no?

**LEO:** Yes. No. I mean, no, we are . . . not.

**SW:** You know you don't have to protect her.

**LEO:** I'm not.

**SW:** Because if you are involved, it's not your fault.

**LEO:** I know.

**SW:** It's got nothing to do with you. There's a whole system designed to deal with exactly this situation.

*(pause)*

**SW:** I'm sorry, why is that funny?

**LEO:** Pardon?

**SW:** You laughed, you smiled just then.

**LEO:** No I didn't. It's just . . . that's exactly what Amy said.

*(pause)*

**SW:** What did she say?

**LEO:** It was nothing.

**SW:** Why would she say that?

**LEO:** I really don't—

**SW:** About a system designed to deal with what? What did she mean, what was she talking about?

**LEO:** Seriously?

**SW:** Seriously.

*(pause)*

**LEO:** If I told you that we . . . I'm not saying we were, I'm just asking . . . if we were . . . what would happen?

**SW:** That depends what you say.

**LEO:** What will happen to me?

**SW:** I'll be honest with you, it will be difficult. You'll have to tell us in detail. What you did, when you did it. It will be uncomfortable, painful. But we'll support you every step of the way to tell your story the way you want to tell it. With all the information and support you need. And if you're not comfortable speaking with me—

**LEO:** You're all right.

*(pause)*

**SW:** It's not your fault, Leo.

*(pause)*

**LEO:** I don't want to get anyone into trouble.

**SW:** People get themselves into trouble.

**LEO:** And I don't want to be in trouble either.

**SW:** That's not what I'm here for. I'm here to help you. If that's what you want.

*(pause)*

**SW:** How long was it going on?

**LEO:** Three months.

**Chat: Leo, 2005557764**
**Friday, April 14, 9 p.m.**

**2005557764:** Have you calmed down yet? Can we actually talk about this like adults?

**2005557764:** Leo, I'm serious. If you want to be in an adult relationship, you have to stop acting like a child.

**2005557764:** I know we can work this out. In private, away from everyone. Just us two.

**2005557764:** Just you and me. Together. On the same team.

**2005557764:** Come on, babe.

**2005557764:** Please

**2005557764:** I don't know why you're acting like this

**2005557764:** You're being such a dick

**2005557764:** It wasn't that serious between us anyway

**2005557764:** Leo

**2005557764:** Leo please reply we need to talk

**2005557764:** Leo

"You tell them when you're ready," I said in his ear. "But you have to tell them. You owe it to yourself. And to her."

He nodded sadly.

"I thought about it."

"Good."

"I even recorded some of what she said in the car."

"Wow. As evidence?"

"Yeah, but I deleted it."

We sat in silence and contemplated relationships, evidence, and deleting things.

"She's not nice," he said, eventually.

---

***Retrieved Voice Recording [Transcript]***
***Friday, April 14, 7:10 p.m.***

*(sound of traffic)*

**LEONARD PRINCE:** You're supposed to go back.

**ELIZABETH STARKEY:** Calm down. It was only a goat.

**LEONARD PRINCE:** It belonged to someone.

**ELIZABETH STARKEY:** They let it on the road. What am I supposed to do?

**LEONARD PRINCE:** It might not be dead.

**ELIZABETH STARKEY:** What are you, dense?

**LEONARD PRINCE:** They might need our help.

**ELIZABETH STARKEY:** Leo, if I go back, I'll get a fine.

**LEONARD PRINCE:** So?

**ELIZABETH STARKEY:** And demerit points.

**LEONARD PRINCE:** You're worried about points?

**ELIZABETH STARKEY:** If I lose my license, I won't be able to get to work.

**LEONARD PRINCE:** You're supposed to go back.

**ELIZABETH STARKEY:** You are so selfish.

**LEONARD PRINCE:** We could save its life.

**ELIZABETH STARKEY:** I don't know about you Leo, but my life is more important.

*(pause)*

It's not just the fine.

*(pause)*

We can't be seen together, Leo. You know that.

*(pause)*

Look, babe, I'm sorry, okay? Let's not fight.

*(traffic sounds)*

*(radio comes on)*

*(radio is turned off)*

*(radio is turned back on)*

*(radio is turned off)*

Grow up.

*(pause)*

**LEONARD PRINCE:** Can you stop the car please?

**ELIZABETH STARKEY:** Babe—

**LEONARD PRINCE:** I want to get out.

**ELIZABETH STARKEY:** What, here?

**LEONARD PRINCE:** Now.

**ELIZABETH STARKEY:** No.

**LEONARD PRINCE:** Now!

**ELIZABETH STARKEY:** No!

**LEONARD PRINCE:** So you're forcing me.

**ELIZABETH STARKEY:** What? No! I'm not . . . geez, Leo, you said you wanted to get out of there!

**LEONARD PRINCE:** No I didn't. You did.

**ELIZABETH STARKEY:** I can't just let you out on the freeway, I've got duty of care.

**LEONARD PRINCE:** Then take me back to the ball.

**ELIZABETH STARKEY:** Fuck me.

*(pause)*

Your loss, buddy.

*(pause. Sound of car indicator and tires turning)*

We'll hook up later. When you've calmed down.

*(pause)*

Babe?

**LEONARD PRINCE:** Yeah. Sure.

*I can assure you that I have been punished several times over in verbal lashings, general opprobrium, and severe consequences, including the responsibility to reimburse the owner of the goat for its replacement, and repay my parents for the cost of the ambulance and body disposal, both of which run to three-figure amounts. As a Year 12 student I do not have ready savings and I have been obliged to commence work in my parents' office supplies business to raise the funds. This is an enormous trial for me academically, as it drastically reduces the time available for my studies, as well as being a great social and personal hardship as by nature I am not at all suited to customer service.*

*To further punish Elroy with the loss of his employment under circumstances of disgrace would be to compound my punishment with unnecessary cruelty, as Elroy and my entire family would, rightly, consider my actions responsible for Elroy's fate. As I have demonstrated in this epistle, he is innocent and if anything deserves reward and congratulation for his attempts to bring me and the entire situation under rational control. It is I who deserve punishment, not he. Please act according to your conscience, and allow Elroy the dignity of continued employment, as is his right.*

*Yours sincerely,*

*Vanessa Nguyen*

**Chat: LochNess, Devinitely**
**Friday, April 14, 9:30 p.m.**

**LochNess:** I called them. Forgiven?

**Devinitely:** What did they say?

**LochNess:** I have to pay for a replacement goat

**Devinitely:** Choc-Top is irreplaceable

**LochNess:** And I have to write a poem and recite it at its memorial service

**Devinitely:** RIP

**LochNess:** Forgiven?

**LochNess:** Devvvvvvvvvv

**Devinitely:** Fine. Forgiven

**LochNess:** My parents also want me to do a satanist reformist course

**Devinitely:** Serious?

**LochNess:** No. But yes about the poem. Luckily I'm a brilliant poet. Not just anyone can find rhymes for Choc-Top

## ✉ Gabby Gibson's Email to the Principal—Page 7

The really bad photo that was on my phone was a terrible accident. Truly. I am so so sorry I ever took it. I never meant to take it like that and if I had looked at it properly and in the light I would never have sent it to anyone not even Bianca and Kate. I have apologized like a million times to Amy and my parents and everyone else and the police were really nice to me and let me off with a warning, and I tell you I could have gone to jail for distributing child pornography just through my carelessness and I am never ever going to make that mistake again! That's for sure.

I did only send it to our group chat and lucky the photo didn't get that far and as far as we know everyone has deleted it (especially me). So it's gone, as much as anything can be gone. I learned my lesson in any case.

Please let the Year 11s have their ball at a proper venue next year. It's not their fault I messed everything up.

Best,

Gabby

# AMY'S JOURNAL

So I called my mum. I had to. The others were still going to the after-party where the whole cycle of revelry would reignite, flare, explode, and burn out. Maybe someone else would get rejected or humiliated or laughed at or kissed, but I wouldn't know because I totally would not be there. I escaped the mad chaos of the foyer, where everyone was kissing and hugging and making arrangements to meet up in twenty, saying who's got the bags, where are we going to get changed, and oh my goodness Macca and Crystal are already in jeans. Macca's dad actually swung through the foyer collecting rented suits on wire coat hangers. Classy.

I slipped out, found a quiet place away from all the mayhem, and made the call. One of those calls that starts out with "Please don't freak out, I'm fine," which is the clearest signal to any parent ever that they must freak out NOW because everything is really very much not fine AT ALL. My mum was kind of awesome about it at that point and didn't even ask many questions, except to find out where I was and make sure I was safe. She said she'd be there in half an hour. I leaned against the wall in the shadow, within sight and earshot of the parade of messy kids shouting at one another, climbing into limos and parents' cars. I wasn't part of the crowd anymore and, for once in my life, was really happy to be ignored.

I was just glad it was all over. The pressure of expectation, that weight of having to make sure we had the most perfect night ever, was all gone. Somehow my complete and utter failure in every single respect didn't seem to matter so much. I felt like a winner just for having survived.

"Hey." The voice was so close, I jumped. "Sorry," he said. It was Vanessa's cousin Elroy. Out of his sweaty T-shirt now, in a clean shirt and jeans, still looking a bit harassed. But younger. "Didn't mean to startle you. Was wondering if you've seen Vanessa?"

"Yeah, she's somewhere over there." I pointed toward where Vanessa had stationed herself on the other side of the entrance, with Mr. Chang. "She can't go until the animal ambulance comes."

"That's a thing?"

"I didn't know either."

"They know it's dead, right?"

"I guess that's why they're taking their time."

Friendly smile. He could have left then. It would have been perfectly all right if he had. Friendly acknowledgment, bit of banter, we don't really know each other, this is all weird, just move on. But he didn't. He clearly thought about it and decided to loiter. And then we both spoke at once.

"Hey, I'm sorry—" (Me.)

"Are you okay after—" (Him.)

Confused moment of us both apologizing. Then he let me go first.

"I just hope we didn't get you into too much trouble."

He shrugged. "Hard to know right now. They sent me home early. I'll find out next week if I've still got a job."

"Oh no, seriously? That's terrible."

"It's not your fault."

"Yes it is! I was the one who said it was cake."

"I took it inside. I shouldn't have done that."

"You were just trying to help."

"I knew better. Vanessa . . ." He gave a gesture of hopelessness. "She's always doing weird shit."

"Someone's got to get it done."

"But usually it's not you, is it?"

"No. Not usually."

He leaned against the wall next to me, and I felt our passing encounter was actually becoming something else. We kept on talking. Within about fifteen minutes I found out:

- He's also in Year 12
- Where he goes to school, where he lives, where he hangs out
- He turns eighteen in a month, which makes him a Taurus OF COURSE, not that it means anything
- He's absolutely divine
- It's really easy to talk to someone when you're not trying to impress them.

Then the text came from my mum. She was actually sitting in the car in the driveway, idling, wondering where I was. I could see her, and I didn't want to go.

"That's her," I said. "School ball is officially over."

"So. On a scale of one to ten. How bad was it?"

"I'd say it was probably the worst school ball in the history of the world."

"That bad?"

"That bad."

"Wow. I mean, as a representative of the Pacific Crest, I wish there was something I could do to make it better."

He's flirting. Yes he is. A totally hot guy I just met is flirting with me, and I've never been stinkier or uglier in my whole life.

"You probably wouldn't have to do that much." Here I was, flirting right back.

"Would a kiss do it?" he asked.

WHAT! Yes, he actually said that! And it was delightful because it was so incredibly sexy, confident, and gutsy and yet still supremely respectful and sweet, and I totally could have said no and it would have been fine. But I didn't want to say no. So I said yes.

And he kissed me.

And everything was totally right with the world as we kissed, and he smiled at me, and I blushed like crazy as we swapped numbers, and I ran off to my mum's waiting car.

And this is why at the end of the worst night of my life, when I had totally been to hell and back, I just couldn't stop smiling.

SCHOOL COMMUNITY NEWSLETTER
FROM THE PRINCIPAL'S DESK

Please make welcome Mr. Jorge Lopez, our latest member of the Mathematics faculty. He will be taking over the Year Twelve General Math class for the rest of this year.

I ask the extended school community to refrain from indulging in rumors and innuendo regarding recent staffing changes.

## AMY'S JOURNAL—FRIDAY

So now that it's been two whole weeks, all the drama and scandal have pretty much died down. Starkey has left. Everybody knows why. Leo's been absent. Same thing. At first everyone kept wanting to talk about it, about how she's going to get arrested and probably will go to jail, who is to blame, Leo's no victim, he just got lucky. Honestly. When Macca said that, I blasted him to smithereens. Starkey was Leo's teacher. She was supposed to look after him, and all of us, and instead, she treated him like her personal plaything, and the rest of us like garbage. What Leo did or said or thought doesn't change that. I think people realize it's serious now. Anyway, if they're still saying stupid things about it, they're not saying them around me.

My parents made me and Gabby and her parents meet with a counselor specializing in online safety, which was every bit as dull as it sounds, but the good news is that the image has pretty much disappeared and all that remains is everyone's version of the HILARIOUS yet actually quite serious story, and my own sense of humiliation. Both of which are quickly becoming So Last Week. Also, would you believe Gabby kissed a Year 11 named Angela at the after-party? So I guess her crush on me is history too. Yep, you've got to keep running pretty fast just to stay in the same spot when you're seventeen.

The biggest changes are actually the subtle ones. I've been hanging out with Kate and Bianca a lot less. Not deliberately. Elroy and I have chatted a bit. Turns out we don't have that much in common after all. He's nice, we're friendly, but the rush of romantic thrill on the night of the ball was just that. A rush. A thrill. It's not my life story, and that's okay. I've been spending more time in the library, and Vanessa and Dev usually hang there so there's always someone up for a chat. And I've been thinking more about not just who I am here in the world of school, but who I want to be in the world outside of it. You only get one school ball—and you only get one life. This is it. This is my shot, and I'm going to make it count.

# EPILOGUE

*I say there never was a lively goat*
*As sweet as she whom we have sadly lost.*
*Why she, so full of zest, with choc'late coat*
*Should crumble like her name? I bear the cost.*
*The righteous guilt weighs heavy on my chest,*
*For I destroyed a thing of pure delight.*
*Yet do not dwell, but think of her at rest:*
*An innocent who is now with the light.*
*I wish you well in caprine afterlife,*
*No pet deserves the violence you endured.*
*I hope you're free from trouble, pain, and strife,*
*And here I leave you with these parting words:*
*We know your dignity remains on top,*
*And so, vale, the dearly loved Choc-Top.*

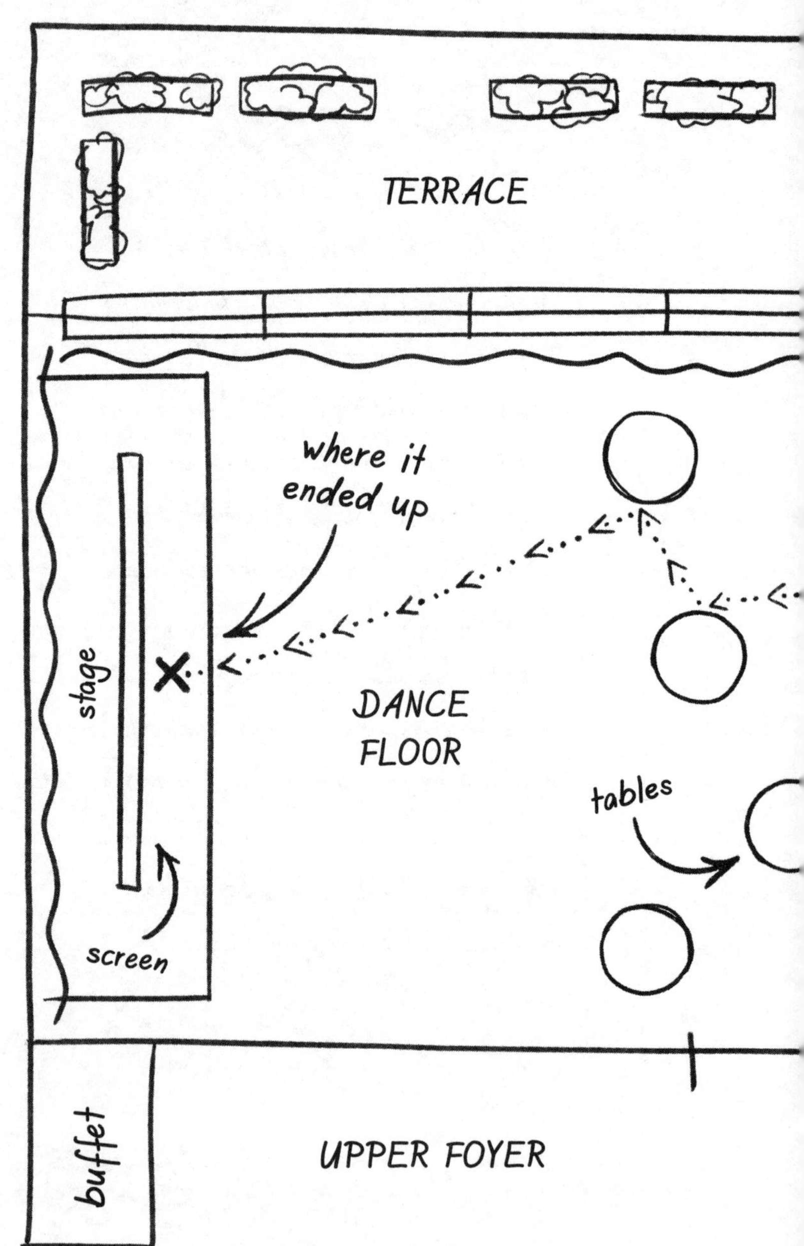
PACIFIC CREST HOTEL – BALLROOM
TERRACE
where it ended up
stage
screen
DANCE FLOOR
tables
buffet
UPPER FOYER

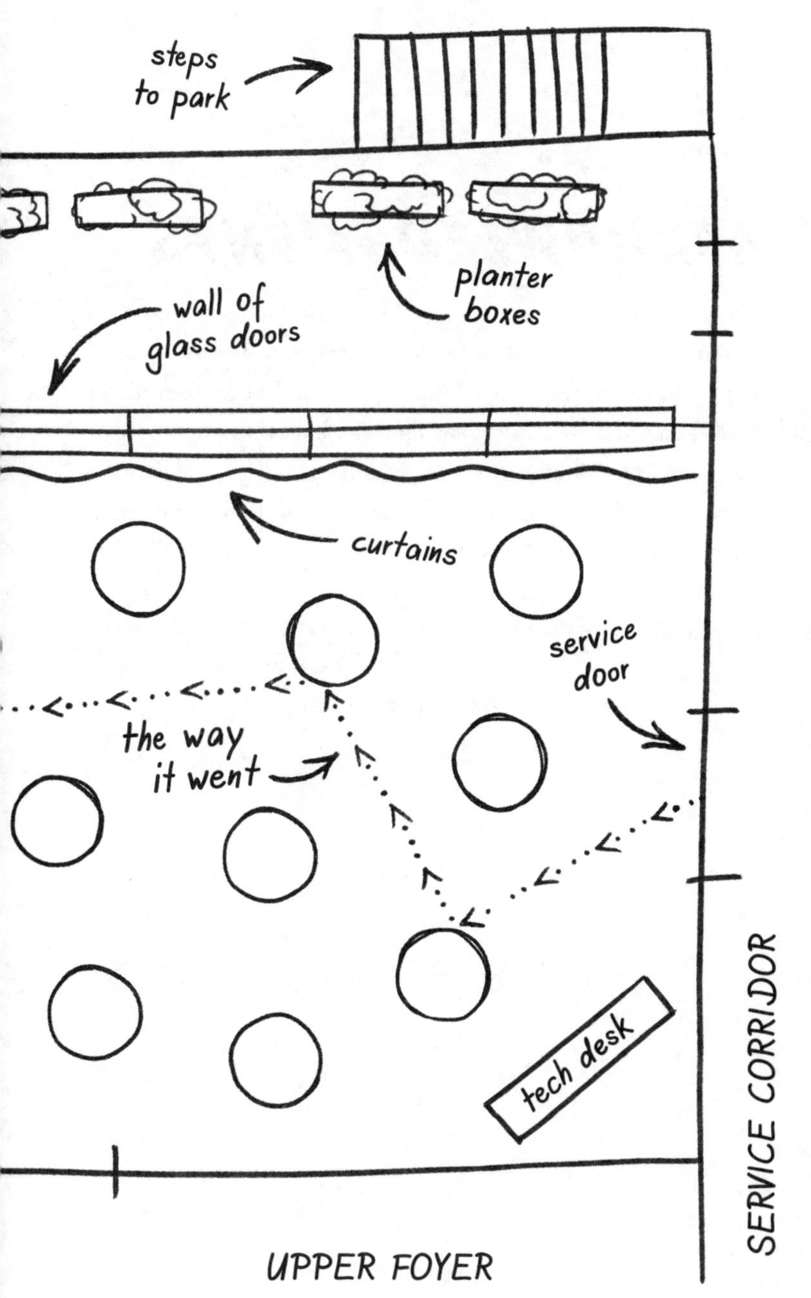

steps
to park
planter
boxes
wall of
glass doors
curtains
service
door
the way
it went
tech desk
SERVICE CORRIDOR
UPPER FOYER

# ACKNOWLEDGMENTS

Thank you once again to Walker Books and Zeitgeist Writers.

Thank you to the teams at CPAM, WME, and Lede, who have shepherded me through many fancy nights in fancy dresses.

Thank you to Jeremy, for letting me sit and watch the first iteration of this story over fifteen years ago, and thank you to Kate, for letting me be a part of it so many years later.

And thank you to Kalliope, because no matter how bad the night is, you always make me feel better.

**—Angourie**

This book is based on a play script that I was commissioned to write for Jeremy Rice, *My Worst Ever Night at the Best School Ball Ever*. Thank you to everyone who participated in its development, including actors Alex Brittan, Cassie Daly, Mischa Ipp, Nicole La Bianca, Rhoda Lopez, Kirsty Marillier, Josh Marshall-Clarke, John Molden, Xavier O'Shannessey, and Clare Regan; designers Cherie Hewson and Patrick Howe; and musicians Katie Campbell and Craig Williams.

Thank you to all who generously gave feedback, including Tiffany Barton, Rose Brown, Christian Leavesley, Belinda Massey, Tahlia Norrish, Maggie Phillips, and Sven Sorensen.

Thank you to the 2010 graduating class of John Curtin College of the Arts, who let us crash their ball for research.

Thank you to Angourie Rice, for taking me and this project where we needed to go. Thank you to Kalliope Rice, who read an early version of the book and kept us on track. And thank you to Jeremy Rice, whose creativity inspires me every single day.

**—Kate**

# RESOURCES

For anyone affected by events and issues similar to those presented in this book, the following organizations offer advice and assistance. If you or anyone you know is in immediate danger, call **911**.

**988 Lifeline** provides all Americans experiencing emotional distress or suicidal thoughts with access to crisis support.

Free
24 hours, 7 days
Call: 988
Text: 988
www.988lifeline.org

**RAINN** provides confidential support services and information to survivors of sexual violence.

Free
24 hours, 7 days
Call: 1-800-656-4673
Text: HOPE to 64673
www.rainn.org

**Childhelp National Child Abuse Hotline** is a national crisis counseling service for those affected by or seeking advice or help related to child abuse.

Free
24 hours, 7 days
Call: 1-800-422-4453
Text: GO to 1-800-422-4453
www.childhelphotline.org

**Love Is Respect** provides information, support, and advocacy for young people between the ages of thirteen and twenty-six who have questions or concerns about their romantic relationships.

Free
24 hours, 7 days
Call: 1-866-331-9474
Text: LOVEIS to 22522
www.loveisrespect.org

**NAMI HelpLine** is a confidential nationwide service that provides emotional support and mental health information and resources needed to tackle challenges that you or your loved ones are facing.

Free
24 hours, 7 days
Call: 1-800-950-6264
Text: NAMI to 62640
www.nami.org